Story
Magic

Story
Magic

Laurel Gale

JOLLY
FiSH
PRESS

Mendota Heights, Minnesota

First Edition
First Printing, 2020

Book design by Sarah Taplin
Cover design by Jake Slavik
Cover illustration by Alison Mutton

Jolly Fish Press, an imprint of North Star Editions, Inc.

Library of Congress Cataloging-in-Publication Data
Names: Gale, Laurel, author.
Title: Story magic / Laurel Gale.
Description: First edition. | Mendota Heights, Minnesota : Jolly Fish Press, [2020] | Audience: Grades 4-6. | Summary: "Twelve-year-old Kaya must harness the power of story magic—ignoring her society's bias against female magic wielders—to save her brother and find herself"— Provided by publisher.
Identifiers: LCCN 2020007628 (print) | LCCN 2020007629 (ebook) | ISBN 9781631634390 (paperback) | ISBN 9781631634406 (ebook)
Subjects: CYAC: Magic—Fiction. | Brothers and sisters—Fiction. | Storytelling—Fiction. | Sex role—Fiction.
Classification: LCC PZ7.1.G347 St 2020 (print) | LCC PZ7.1.G347 (ebook) | DDC [Fic]—dc23
LC record available at https://lccn.loc.gov/2020007628
LC ebook record available at https://lccn.loc.gov/2020007629

Jolly Fish Press
North Star Editions, Inc.
2297 Waters Drive
Mendota Heights, MN 55120
www.jollyfishpress.com

Printed in the United States of America

For James. You know why.

Chapter One

There was a listener nearby. Kaya A'Dor could sense it, the way it made her skin tingle ever so slightly. She knew she wasn't supposed to notice—and she definitely wasn't supposed to do anything about it if she did—but the opportunity tempted her.

See, she'd forgotten to start the bread that morning.

It was because she had stayed up so late the night before. The blanket she was knitting took her longer than expected, a result of the new stitch she was trying, and when she finally woke up the next morning, she wanted to go straight to the market to sell it. No one was buying, though. Bored, she decided to check out the street performers, and the jugglers, dancers, and drummers did a good job of keeping her mind off her empty purse. Too good a job. By the time she finally headed home, it was late afternoon.

Kaya's brother, Hob A'Dor, would return in less than an hour, which didn't leave nearly enough time for the dough to rise.

A little magic from the listeners could fix that.

But according to the Story Magicians Guild, it was bad luck for a girl to attempt magic. It angered the listeners, they claimed. It led to disaster.

Nonsense, Hob had argued. The magicians just wanted to keep women out of the guild. The listeners didn't care about gender any more than they cared about age, social class, or wealth. Only one thing mattered to them: good stories.

Their ma, he added, had dabbled in story magic, though only when their pa wasn't around to witness it.

Kaya wasn't so sure. She didn't remember their ma practicing magic, but that could have been because she'd only been seven when their parents had died, perhaps too young to be trusted with dangerous secrets.

And that was the other problem. The fact that they had died. Their parents had died, so maybe the magicians were right after all. It was bad luck for women and girls to work spells.

But Hob insisted otherwise, and he'd always taken care of her. Orphans would normally have to live—or die—on the streets, but he used his stipend from the Story Magicians Guild to pay for a rented room and a little food for the both of them. When he got back from his work at the guild each day, he passed on some of what he had learned, teaching Kaya how to sense listeners and even how to summon them.

He'd be proud to come home and discover that she'd worked her first spell. He'd be disappointed to find out that there was no bread to go with dinner.

Kaya hated disappointing him.

It wouldn't have to be a very strong spell. Just something to speed up the rising process.

She'd never told a story before. As a very young child, before learning good sense, she'd started a few, but her pa had always hushed her before she could finish. Only members of the guild were allowed to tell stories, and stories told for amusement were strictly forbidden. They would confuse the listeners, or so the guild warned, and no one wanted that.

Kaya had never told a story, but she had listened to the ones her brother told. She'd thought about them too.

"Listeners," she began, her squeaky voice barely more than a whisper—a good thing, in case the landlord was eavesdropping on the other side of the thin walls. "I have a story that may interest you."

The tingling sensation on the back of her neck intensified. The listener was listening.

"Once," she began, "a long time ago, in a faraway place, there lived a girl named Kay—uh—Kalla. Yes. There lived a girl named Kalla . . . uh, just Kalla. See, she, uh, she lived alone. In fact, she was the only person in her entire world. And it was a horrible world, too, an awful world because . . . because . . . because . . ."

Kaya didn't know what to say next. Her eyes watered. Her heart pounded. Sweat slicked her palms. Hob had always made magic look so easy, but this wasn't easy at all.

What had she been thinking? She was a girl. It was bad luck. Besides, she doubted she could create a tale on the spot, the way real magicians did, the way Hob did.

The tingling on her neck faded. The listener was getting bored. Soon, it would get angry.

Kaya tried to recall some of the stories Hob had told, but she couldn't think of any that would work. It wouldn't have mattered anyway. Listeners didn't care for repeats.

They cared even less for unfinished stories. You couldn't address a listener and then not satisfy it. Everyone knew that. Not even Hob disputed it. The invisible beings held great power, and they were not to be annoyed.

Kaya needed a story.

She needed it to include words that could make the bread rise.

What had she said already? The world in the story was horrible because . . . because . . . because . . .

"Because it was always night there!" she said—yelled, really, excited that an idea had finally come to her. In a lowered voice, she continued. "Kalla had never seen the sun. She didn't even know it existed."

The pleasant tingling returned. The listener was happy—for now.

"So Kalla was very sad and lonely because she had no light and no friends. There were only blood wolves that hunted in packs and spiders that crawled at her feet, and she was always scared and cold.

"One day—uh, *night*, I mean, because it was always night—a visitor came to her world. He was Hom, a generous man, and he had the power to control the skies. 'Rise!' he said, and the sun rose. Kalla's world became bright and beautiful, and it was warm and wonderful, and Hom stayed on the planet to take care of the girl forever and ever. The end."

Kaya held her breath and waited for a reaction. There was none, of course. She knew better than to expect applause. The listeners weren't like the crowds at the market. They didn't cheer or clap, no matter how good the performance was. If the listener accepted her story, it would show its appreciation by giving power to her words.

"Rise," she said, looking at the lump of dough.

The dough expanded to nearly three times its original size. It floated upward, too, levitating above the table for several seconds before gently falling back down.

The listener had liked her story.

Chapter Two

Hob slammed the door, a bad habit the landlord had complained about on numerous occasions. Apparently, the ceiling could collapse at any moment, and the added stress of a rough entrance might hasten the disaster.

Sometimes Kaya lost sleep worrying about the unstable roof over her head. Stormy nights frightened her the most. If Hob's temper could damage their home, then surely a strong gust of wind or heavy downpour of rain could obliterate it. She didn't even want to think about what would happen if lightning struck.

"Is dinner ready?" he demanded in lieu of a greeting. No one who wasn't family could have gotten away with such rudeness, but Kaya had grown so accustomed to it that she barely noticed.

Perhaps she let him get away with even more because he was the only family she had. They had lived together since her birth, which meant she knew her brother better than she knew anyone else, even her parents who had died five years ago.

They had gotten sick. Hob had asked for the guild's help, but he was a only new apprentice, and his requests weren't considered a priority. By the time the guild finally sent a magician over, it was too late. Their parents had succumbed to their illness, and Hob blamed the guild. He'd wanted to quit, but the apprenticeship was all they had left. He stuck it out— for Kaya.

Hob looked like her, with the same light-olive skin and straight brown hair. Their eyes were equally big, their noses equally thin. Hob was seven years older than Kaya, though, and nearly twice as big. He had an appetite to match his size.

He was wearing a green tunic with the image of a broad-leafed plant—the conjuring herb—embroidered on it. It was an outfit that marked him as a guild apprentice and filled Kaya with pride. The guild didn't accept just anyone, but Hob had been accepted when he was only twelve. Kaya, currently twelve years old herself, had never accomplished anything half as impressive, her recent spell included.

In a few years, his apprenticeship would end. Then he'd be Hob Im'Dor, a full-fledged magician. Kaya wouldn't be Kaya A'Dor, a name that marked her as an orphan forever. When she grew old enough to marry, she would become Kaya Li'Dor, a member of the lower class. Or, in the unlikely event that she married a man in the upper class, she would become Kaya S'Dor. But women could not be magicians, so she would never be Kaya Im'Dor, no matter how much magic she managed.

"Bread's baking and stew's warming." She gestured to the wood-burning oven that occupied one corner of their single room. It served the dual purpose of cooking their food and keeping them warm. She took a deep breath, eager to tell her brother the big news. "I used story magic today. I sensed a listener the way you taught me to, and I told it a story about a hero who made the sun rise, and then I told the dough to rise, and it did."

"Good."

That was less of a response than Kaya had been hoping for. Her brother was probably just tired, which was understandable after a long day.

"I was thinking," Kaya said, speaking too quickly. "Can't I create a story that ends with the magic words 'and then a million gold coins appeared'? Then the listeners would give us the coins, right?"

Hob dismissed her with a wave of his hand. "Don't be ridiculous. The listeners make things *happen*. They don't *make* things. They don't create anything. They can transport coins to you, but only by stealing them from someone else, and then people would demand to know where you got the coins."

"Then what about something else?" Kaya asked. "An ox, maybe." An animal like that would be worth a lot of money.

"Same problem," Hob said. "You can get an ox to walk over to you, but you can't get an ox to appear out of the void. And if you bring over someone else's ox, you'll be accused of theft, same as if you'd taken it any other way. You have to use your head about these things."

"Sorry," Kaya said, although she didn't see what was ridiculous about wanting gold coins so they could rent a better apartment, one with a good roof and furniture that didn't wobble and creak, or so she could buy a decent pair of shoes and some cloth to make a new dress.

Hob's stipend from the Story Magicians Guild was enough to cover the rent for their tiny home and keep them from starving, but not much else. Kaya earned what she could, too, but hardly anyone wanted to buy blankets from a young girl these days. If they were poor, they knitted their own. If they were rich, they got special ones made from silk and imported from faraway lands.

So, of course, she'd like to make some gold coins appear.

And what was "ridiculous" about not knowing how magic worked? Hob only knew because he got to study at the fancy guild. He had probably asked a similar question himself when he started training.

"If listeners can convince an ox to walk over to you, could they convince the ox's owner to give you the ox? Or all his money?" Kaya wasn't sure she'd want to do that—it might still be stealing—but maybe if the owner was a bad enough man, it would be okay.

Hob shook his head. "I've tried spells like that, but listeners can't seem to manipulate the minds of people—only the minds of animals. Either that, or they *won't* do it. I think there are a lot of things listeners could do, if they wanted, if we could only make them."

Kaya wasn't sure she understood that. People got the listeners to do magic by telling stories. There was no other way to make the invisible creatures do anything, not that Kaya knew of. She could see that her questions were irritating Hob, though.

"It was fun to work a spell," she said. "I almost couldn't think of a story, and then I was afraid the listener wouldn't like it enough to give my words magic, but the dough didn't merely rise—it floated above the table too!"

"Uh-huh," he mumbled. His eyes had a distant look to them. "How long until dinner's ready?"

"A few minutes, I think. Aren't you proud?" She'd expected more excitement for her first spell. "You said you wanted me to try magic, that I shouldn't be afraid just because the guild says listeners don't like girls."

"Oh, yeah, sorry." He smiled and squeezed Kaya's hand. "Like I said, it's good. I'm proud of you. I'm just not surprised. I always knew you could do it. The guild tries to pretend it's hard, something only a chosen few should attempt, but that's only because they're afraid of losing power. Anyone with half a brain can do story magic."

Kaya thought her story had taken more than half a brain to tell. She didn't say that, though, because she didn't want to argue and she could see that Hob was in a bad mood. "Did everything go well today?"

"No. I got into another fight with Ace Im'Ref."

Ace was the most powerful magician in Verdan—more than powerful enough to kick Hob out of the guild. Kaya gulped. "What about?"

"Same old stuff. I want the guild to help out more. The harvests have been bad this year, and people need food. The magicians could make the grain grow faster, instead of focusing so much on growing conjuring herb. And the hospital that burned down last year still hasn't been rebuilt. Magicians could help build a school and a couple of orphanages while they're at it, but Ace refuses."

Kaya's eyes widened at the mention of a school. She'd always wanted to attend classes, the way some of the kids in the capital city, Prima, did. But she knew she shouldn't get excited. Even if Verdan ever built a school—a big *if*—there was no way girls would be allowed to attend. "Why won't Ace help?"

"He says it's complicated, that there are problems I don't know about because I'm only an apprentice. But I know more than he realizes." He hesitated, then shrugged. "The guild has never wanted to practice too much magic around poor folk. They worry that people will see how easy it is and start doing it for themselves. Then the guild won't be so powerful anymore."

Kaya remembered how nervous she'd felt when her story had faltered. "It's not that easy. And most people don't know how to sense listeners."

"It's not that hard to learn, not half as hard as the guild wants people to think. They're not as important as they claim, and people are going to realize that. There are ways to power that don't involve the guild. Grey and I have heard about a group—"

"Do you smell something burning?" Kaya interrupted. Before her brother could answer, she raced to the oven.

Her beautiful loaf of bread had burned.

"It's fine," Hob said. "I'm so hungry I don't care what rubbish you feed me."

Kaya nodded. "Some of it's still good. I'll eat the black parts." She couldn't help feeling disappointed, though, and it wasn't just because the rising cost of flour made the burned loaf expensive. She'd worked story magic to make that bread. It had been a successful spell—her very first—and now it was rubbish.

Maybe it *was* bad luck for a girl to use magic after all.

Chapter Three

*T*wo weeks later, Kaya passed the time by knitting another blanket. She doubted she'd be able to sell it—none of the others she'd knitted had sold in months—but there was nothing else to do. The floor was swept. The evening's dinner was ready. Hob should have been home over an hour ago, but he was late. Again.

Sometimes magicians kept themselves busy by working spells. They told silly stories to make drums play themselves or to make candles dance. It was supposed to be good practice.

Kaya didn't sense any listeners nearby, but she could always summon one. Hob had left her some sticks of the conjuring incense that attracted them, even though the guild would punish him if they learned he was giving it to nonmembers. Apprentices weren't even allowed to possess the precious sticks outside the guild's fields and the guildhall.

Hob was taking a huge risk by disobeying, but he didn't seem to care. Kaya, who didn't think she could ever do anything so daring, admired his bravery. She was grateful for it too. After all, he was doing it for her.

If she burned some of the incense, a listener would come. She could tell a story to make the yarn knit itself into a blanket.

Or she could create a tale to fix the leak that had sprung in the roof. The autumn nights were cold enough without rain dripping on them while they slept. Hob kept promising to fix the leak with some story magic of his own, but he'd been too busy recently to find time. At least, that was the excuse he kept giving Kaya. More than once, he'd suggested she could tell a story to fix it, and she suspected that was his real reason for putting it off. He wanted her to do it.

She'd cast her first spell a fortnight ago, and she still hadn't worked up the courage to try another.

The bread had burned.

Sure, it could have been because she'd added too much wood to the fire or because Hob's rant had gone on too long, but that didn't mean there wasn't another cause as well. Girls weren't supposed to practice story magic.

Some said it was because girls weren't smart enough. Their weak, uncreative minds would lead to weak, uncreative stories, the types of tales that listeners wouldn't tolerate. Others said it was because girls weren't clean enough. The listeners, being pure creatures, did not want to be sullied by a female presence, no matter how good the stories were. And others claimed that the reason was beyond human understanding. The listeners simply didn't like girls, and it was not anyone's place to question that.

While people debated the reason, they agreed on the result. Girls who told stories suffered for it.

If a girl drowned, it was whispered that she'd been dabbling in magic, and a listener had held her under the water as punishment. If a woman coughed up blood, no one doubted that she'd been telling tales.

It wasn't just the female storytellers themselves who would suffer. Ill-tempered listeners could strike down entire houses to punish a single girl. They might even destroy whole towns if too many girls dared tell tales. When rodents ate a family's grain supply, or when a plague spread, female storytellers were usually to blame.

Hob dismissed it as superstitious rumor, but what if he was wrong?

If the burned loaf was a punishment, it was a very small one. But what if it was only a warning? What if the next punishment was worse?

Kaya kept knitting.

The door opened, then slammed shut after Hob entered. Some dirt fell from the ceiling, which was better than the ceiling itself falling.

"The guild's really working you hard," Kaya said. She got a bowl of stew and some bread ready for him. The piece of bread was smaller than usual—it was becoming difficult to buy grain, even for those who had some coins set aside—but the serving of stew was extra big to make up for it.

Hob stuffed the small piece of bread into his mouth and swallowed it with hardly any chewing. "Huh? Oh, yeah, it's gotten late, hasn't it? I wasn't with the guild. I was at The Crusty Loaf."

While technically a restaurant, The Crusty Loaf served as a meeting place for Verdan's miscreants. It wasn't like her brother to waste the little money they had patronizing that sort of establishment, but he must have had a reason. "Were you with someone?"

A girl, maybe. That would explain the late hours recently. At nineteen, Hob was still a little young to marry, but Kaya wouldn't mind having a sister-in-law around. Unless the sister-in-law felt differently. Hob's new wife might not want to share her home with a pesky kid, especially not when all they had was an already-cramped apartment.

Then where would Kaya go? She had an aunt and an uncle in Prima, the giant city to the north, but she'd never met them, and there was no reason to think they would welcome an extra mouth to feed. Kaya would find herself out on the streets.

But Hob would never allow that. He'd always taken care of her.

"Grey," Hob said, his mouth full of bread. He meant Grey Li'Dag, his best friend. "And MAGE."

"Mage?" It wasn't a name Kaya had ever heard of her before. "Who's she?"

"Not she. It. Magicians Advocating Gain for Everyone. M-A-G-E. MAGE." He lowered his voice to a whisper. "It's a secret group that aims to limit the power of the guild and make magic available to everyone."

Kaya froze, unable to swallow the stew she had in her mouth. After a moment, she spat it out. "Did you and Grey start it?"

"No. They've been around for years, but we just joined last week." He pulled up his sleeve to reveal a piece of blue yarn that he'd tied around his wrist. "They wear this so they can recognize each other wherever they go. See, they're not just here in Verdan. They've got branches everywhere. Well, not Silenton, but most places. They're in Prima, of course. Not that you could tell, though, based on how little they've accomplished. They know things about the guild—secrets that could lead to the guild's downfall—but they're not doing anything about it. Good thing I'm a member now. I've got an idea that will change everything."

He continued eating his meal, as casually as if they'd just had a conversation about the weather, but Kaya had lost her appetite.

Hob had always criticized the guild. He'd broken the rules, too, sneaking home conjuring incense and teaching Kaya lessons on the sly. This was different, though. He'd joined some sort of rebel group and was talking about taking the guild down.

If Hob got caught, he would be exiled from the guild, maybe even the kingdom. Assuming he wasn't imprisoned. Assuming he wasn't executed. The guild held a great deal of power—some said they rivaled the king himself—and they'd crush anyone who threatened them in order to keep it that way.

Chapter Four

Kaya kept going to the market nearly every day. With Hob spending more and more time at MAGE meetings, the tiny apartment seemed lonelier and lonelier. At least at the market, she could talk to people and watch the street performers. She hoped to sell something, too, though the chance of that seemed slim. She had six blankets with her, and they were her very best, but despite the icy wind, no one wanted them.

Maybe they'd look more appealing wrapped around her than folded into tidy squares. People would see how big they were, how fine the knitting was. And even if no one cared, at least she'd stay warm.

"Blankets!" she shouted, wrapping a couple of them around herself with as much fanfare as she could manage.

A woman glanced at the blankets. Her dress was plain, but it wasn't overly dirty or worn, so she might have a few coins to spare.

"They make beautiful shawls, too," Kaya said. "Buy one before they sell out."

The woman continued without stopping, as did the next dozen who passed.

Maybe it was the location. Kaya moved on in search of a better spot.

A couple of blocks down, people seemed to be in less of a hurry. An old man played a pipe while a younger man kept the rhythm with a small drum. Across the street, a woman sold rustberry jam, and a boy offered to clean people's shoes. There was enough room between them for another person. None of their offerings competed with hers, and the music was nice. Kaya decided this was as good a spot as any to spend the day.

Before sitting, she had to shoo away a large group of birds. Dirt-doves, most people called them, because their grayish-brown feathers had a perpetually filthy appearance. Other people called them orphans, because they looked dirty and were normally found living on the street. Kaya didn't like that nickname for them.

Some of the dirt-doves returned, but when they saw that Kaya didn't have any food, they flew off again.

There used to be even more of the birds around. Then, about the same time the crops failed and food became scarce, their numbers dwindled. Maybe they were simply starving like everyone else, but Kaya was suspicious of some of the so-called chicken that had been showing up at the butcher's recently.

More people passed her, sometimes on foot, sometimes on horseback, and occasionally in carriages. Kaya shouted about her blankets to all of them.

After an hour or so, someone responded.

"What beautiful blankets!" the girl said. She was slightly older than Kaya, but shorter and less scrawny, and her thick braid of auburn hair reached her lower back. "Such fine knitting!"

Kaya smiled, but she didn't bother to stand. The girl was Anny Li'Fab, her friend, and she sat beside Kaya.

Anny sold ribbons that her ma made—or, at least, she tried. Ribbons were even less popular than blankets. Luckily, though, Anny's pa earned a decent wage as a smith's assistant, and although a little extra coin would help, it wasn't needed for survival.

"Want to borrow a blanket?" Kaya asked, because Anny's teeth were chattering in the chilly breeze. "I'm trying to show that they work as shawls too. You can model it for me. This blue one will look good on you."

"Thanks," Anny said, accepting the blanket eagerly. "I can braid a couple of ribbons into your hair."

Kaya turned around so Anny could do that.

Kaya's ma used to braid her hair every day, back before she died. Since then, Kaya had worn her hair down, even though it got tangled that way.

"I might be getting an apprenticeship," Anny said.

"That's wonderful!" Apprenticeships were rare, especially for girls. They were valuable too. The Story Magicians Guild was in charge of farming, among other things, and only the upper class could own land, so it was hard for people in the lower class to earn a living. They had to find something to make and sell, or some service to perform, if they wanted to earn enough coin to survive. An apprenticeship could lead to a nice job that paid well.

"Not that wonderful. It's to be an embroiderer, and I hate embroidery. My parents are setting it up."

"I think it sounds fun," Kaya said. "Maybe you can show me some of what you learn."

"Yeah, maybe." Anny's fingers tugged on a knot in Kaya's hair. "Did you hear about the S'Weeps? Their house burned down. I heard it's because a listener was unhappy about a bad story."

"Or because it's been cold and windy, and a fire they started to keep warm grew out of control," Kaya said. Kaya hadn't heard about the fire, but it was no surprise that Anny had. Anny always managed to learn every word of gossip that spread through Verdan. "Did anyone survive?"

"No. Things like this make me wonder if the Silent are right."

The Silent were people who thought the listeners were evil. Kaya had never met one, but Anny had told her all about them.

"Hob would know if the listeners were bad," Kaya said.

"Perhaps. Does he know if the rumors about the guild are true?"

"What rumors?"

"The listeners have abandoned the guild," Anny said. "That's why there's not much food. The crops aren't growing as well without the listeners' help."

"Hob hasn't said anything." Although he did mention secrets that could lead to guild's downfall. Could this be what he meant? Kaya decided not to say anything. If people suspected that the guild had lost its power and could no longer help people, unrest would follow. That wouldn't help anyone. Besides, it sounded like another silly rumor.

Anny finished the braid. "There's a hole in your dress. Your hair was covering it before I braided it. Do you want me to undo it?"

"No, leave it." There was another hole near Kaya's left armpit, and two more in the skirt, so concealing one hardly seemed worth the effort. She needed to patch them but had run out of material, and all the extra money Hob had given her had been spent on yarn to make blankets that wouldn't sell.

"Okay. How is Hob?"

"Fine," Kaya said, sounding a little curter than she'd meant to.

They sat for a while. Normally, they would chat about the street performers or more of the gossip Anny had heard, but today Kaya remained silent. She could only think of one topic—Hob's activity with MAGE—and that was not something she could discuss with anyone, not even Anny.

Especially not Anny. There were downsides to having a friend who liked to gossip.

After a few minutes, a boy approached them. Kaya didn't recognize him, which meant he couldn't be a regular at the market. She wondered where he came from. Verdan was a small town, known only for the guild-controlled fields of grain and conjuring herb. The boy could have been the son of a magician, recently moved to help with the year's poor harvest. He could belong to a group of wanderers, those people whose penchant for robbery and tricks made staying in one place a dangerous proposition. Or perhaps he wasn't new to Verdan at all, but simply didn't appear in the market often. He might be the son of a baker, or of a maid, or any number of possibilities. His clothes were plain but clean and revealed little of his status.

"Are you selling much?" he asked. Kaya couldn't tell whether he was interested in selling or in buying.

"No," Anny said.

"Yes," Kaya lied, in case he was interested in buying. "These blankets are very popular. If you want one, you'd better get it now."

He eyed the tight knitting and nodded. "Okay. But it's not for me. I'm scouting out fine items for a wealthy upper-class lady. I think she'd be interested in your blankets."

A wealthy lady! If she liked them well enough, she might convince her friends to buy them too. Kaya could make a small fortune if she started selling to the upper class.

"Does she want some ribbons too?" Anny asked.

"No, just the blankets. Come with me so she can see them." He waved Kaya forward. She stood and started toward him.

Anny stopped her. "You need this," she said, taking off the borrowed blanket.

"No, you keep it. I have more than enough to sell." Hopefully the lady wouldn't want the one Kaya was wearing. Kaya hadn't been thinking about how dirty it would get when she sat on the ground.

"You can keep the ribbons too." Anny smiled. "They look nice in your hair. Maybe the lady will decide she wants them after seeing them."

Kaya thanked Anny before continuing after the boy. When she had almost caught up to him, he raced forward several paces, always staying ahead of her. She kept chasing him, and soon she found herself in a part of the market she generally avoided. Called the Shadows, it was known for shady business dealings, illicit products, and frequent fights.

It was not the sort of place where a wealthy lady would go to buy blankets.

The boy was a wanderer. Kaya should have known better than to follow him—and would have, if she hadn't been blinded by the promise of money.

She turned around. If she was quiet enough, maybe the boy wouldn't notice that she'd stopped following, at least not until she was back with Anny on the busy main street.

"Where you going?" another boy asked. He must have sneaked up behind Kaya. Now he was standing right in front of her. He looked exactly like the first boy—a twin.

Make that triplets. Quadruplets. She was surrounded.

On second glance, she saw that the two boys looming on either side of her resembled neither each other nor the first pair. They weren't related to the twins—which didn't make them any less threatening or her any less trapped. They had gotten her alone so she'd be easier to rob.

"Give us your blankets," one of them ordered.

"Give us your purse," another added.

She'd gone to the market to sell, not to buy, and despite what she'd told the boy, she hadn't been successful. She kept a small coin purse in her pocket, but she didn't have any money in it. If she let these boys take her blankets, she wouldn't get any, either.

Her skin tingled. A listener had arrived. Was it a coincidence, or did they enjoy real-life action as much as they did stories? Hob would know, but he wasn't there. Kaya was on her own.

She had only one means of defending herself: story magic. It had worked before, burned bread aside.

Hob would want her to tell the story. In fact, he would be angry if she told him she'd let these boys take her blankets—made with the yarn he'd paid for—because she was too afraid to try another story.

"Listeners," she whispered under her breath, "I have a story that may interest you."

"What did you say?" the nearest boy demanded.

"Once, there was a girl named Kanna," she continued. The prickly sensation on the back of her neck grew stronger, letting her know that the listener was listening. "And she was weak and helpless, so mean people tormented her. One day, she made, uh, blankets. No, not blankets. She made . . . uh . . . uh . . . okay, blankets. But they were special blankets. She worked the yarn in such a way that they shimmered like gold. And people loved them, but they didn't think they could afford anything so lovely, so she never sold any."

"What's she blabbering about?" one of the boys asked.

"I think she's doing story magic!" another answered.

The first boy's eyes widened. "But she's a girl."

"Make her stop!"

"You can't interrupt a story. It's bad luck!"

"So's letting a girl do story magic!"

They stepped toward her.

"If you interrupt the story," she warned them, taking a step backward, "the listener will attack you." She continued her story. "Then one day, an evil goblin stole the blankets from Kanna. See, the goblin thought the blankets were really made of gold. He was a greedy goblin, never satisfied with what he had, so he stole Kanna, too, and forced her to make more blankets day and night until her fingers bled from knitting so much. Kanna would have been doomed to toil away forever, but she had a brother named, uh, Holl, who had heard of the greedy goblin and knew the evil creature must have taken Kanna. Holl was determined to rescue her. See, Holl could, uh . . . he could, uh . . ."

"Get her to stop speaking!" one of the twins yelled.

"You do it!" his twin yelled back. They weren't getting any closer to her.

Kaya had planned to have the hero summon a sword to fight the goblin, but that was silly because she didn't know how to wield a sword. Besides, her brother had said the listeners couldn't make things appear out of nothing. They could cause an ox to wander over, but she didn't see how an ox would help—although she wouldn't want to be kicked by one, and a stampede sounded absolutely horrifying.

Maybe the listeners could bring her a sword, but it would belong to someone else. Kaya didn't want to steal, and it would be especially hypocritical now. And again, she wouldn't know how to use it.

"We should leave," one of the other boys said. "I don't want to mess with the listeners."

Kaya hoped they would leave, although they seemed too curious to move. Either way, she still had to finish her story. A sword wouldn't work, she decided, and neither would an ox, but maybe another animal would. She didn't have any other ideas at the moment, so it would have to do. "Holl had befriended all the birds, and they would do as he asked. He said, 'Come, birds, and offer your protection.' All sorts of birds swarmed the skies. Afraid of being pecked to death, the goblin ran away, and Holl took Kanna to safety. The end."

She took a deep breath. "Come, birds, and offer your protection."

Nothing happened. The four boys looked at each other, then at Kaya. They stepped toward her.

A dozen dirt-doves swooped down on the boys.

Chapter Five

The dirt-doves kept coming. Other birds joined as well: a horned vulture, a couple of gray crows, and a few city sparrows. The boys screamed, and the sound blended with the caws, coos, and chirps.

Amid the chaos of flapping wings, Kaya made her escape.

The boys hadn't tried to harm her. They'd only wanted her blankets and some money, no doubt so they could stay warm and fed. Kaya hadn't needed to hurt them. She should have come up with a story that would . . . that would . . . well, she wasn't sure what else she could have done, but there had to have been something.

Or she could have just handed over her blankets and her empty purse. It wasn't as if they were doing her much good, and it would have been a lot smarter than trying to work another spell. But she'd wanted to impress Hob. Why had she thought he'd be impressed by such foolishness?

She'd done story magic—in public. Not even Hob would be that brazen in his disregard for the guild's rules. He wouldn't be proud of her. He'd be horrified. What had she been thinking?

Most of the birds were following her, but some of them had stayed behind to torment the boys.

The boys had realized she was doing story magic. It was obvious, really. Once they got away from the birds, they could report her to the guild. They probably wouldn't, due to their being criminals and therefore not too friendly with the authorities, but it was still a risk. They might turn her in. Or someone else might. Anyone could notice the birds following her around and figure out that something strange was afoot.

There was no way of knowing how long the spell would last. Minutes. Hours. Most spells didn't last any longer than a day at most, but some could go on for longer. Since her story hadn't specified a length, it would depend on the will of the listener. In the meantime, Kaya needed to lie low. She went home.

—

Late that evening, Kaya reminded herself that there was no reason to worry. These days, it was normal for Hob to return late. It didn't mean that the guild had detained him to ask how his little sister had learned to summon birds. He was probably at another MAGE meeting or else wasting time griping with Grey about all the injustices in the world.

But there were still dirt-doves cooing outside their home, which made not worrying difficult, no matter how much Kaya told herself not to.

Maybe Hob had gotten sick from the questionable food served at The Crusty Loaf. Or he'd gotten mugged on his way home. He'd fought back, being as brave as he was, but the muggers had outnumbered him, and now he was lying injured in some alley.

Whatever had happened, it was her fault. Everyone knew girls couldn't do magic without causing bad luck. Her first story had resulted in a burned loaf. Her second story might have resulted in something much worse.

Heated for too long, the stew had turned into an unpalatable mush. Kaya had lost her appetite anyway.

Hob could be in trouble because of her story magic. He might need help. The autumn night was even colder than the autumn afternoon had been, so Kaya grabbed a blanket before heading outside.

Only a few dirt-doves followed her, not as many as she'd feared. The sun had set, and the streets were nearly deserted. The half-moon and the stars provided a little light, but she probably should have brought the lamp. She hadn't thought of it, though, because on the rare occasions that she went out at night, she was always with Hob, who used story magic to light their path.

Closer to The Crusty Loaf, the streets became less empty. The restaurant itself was full of people and light and warmth. Kaya peered inside the open door but didn't see her brother anywhere. She walked away.

"Hey!" a man said. He had short hair and a beard, a common style among young men his age. "You sell blankets at the market, don't you?"

Was he interested in buying? Or did he recognize her as the girl who had performed story magic? Not wanting to take any risks, she shook her head. "You must be thinking of someone else."

A group of young women approached the entrance, nearly knocking Kaya to the ground as they pushed their way past her. They were probably just rude, but they might have been pickpockets trying to get close enough to steal some coins. If so, they didn't get the chance. A couple of dirt-doves pecked at their hair. Swatting the birds away, the women hurried into the restaurant.

The man who'd asked about the blankets eyed Kaya, who sensed suspicion in his gaze. He knew what she'd done.

She looked inside the restaurant one more time—still no sign of her brother—before fleeing.

No more birds followed her. Which was good—that suspicious man might not have been the only person watching her—but it didn't *feel* good. The night was dark, and she was by herself. The winged pests had frightened her, but they had also protected her. Now that they were gone, she felt vulnerable.

She didn't need animals to keep her safe, though. She needed her brother.

Maybe Grey would know where to find Hob. Kaya hadn't seen Grey at The Crusty Loaf, but she knew where he lived. She headed there.

—

Grey had his own rented room. Not because he was an orphan like Kaya and Hob, but because he'd gotten into too many fights with his parents and had moved out of their house at the first opportunity. To Kaya, this made him something of a dolt. Sure, his parents might not have been perfect, but they were family. Why anyone would choose to live alone in a rundown shack of a room was beyond her.

The door was open. She knocked anyway.

Grey came to the door carrying a bag. He was tall and thin, almost gaunt, with brown hair in need of a trim. His face, scarred from too many fistfights, wrinkled in confusion. "What are you doing here?"

"Do you know where Hob is?" Kaya asked. "He hasn't come home. Is he here?"

"He's gone. The two of us should get gone too."

Kaya felt sick. She'd been right. Something bad had happened. "What do you mean? Where is Hob?"

"The guild knows what he's been doing," Grey said. "But it's all right. We have a plan."

Kaya still didn't understand. "What kind of plan? Is Hob in danger? Are you going to help him?"

Grey shook his head. "I wish I could, but it's too dangerous, and I have other things to do. The guild won't be powerful for much longer."

"I don't care about that! I just want to find Hob. You said the guild knows . . ." Her eyes watered, and her voice cracked. "Did the guild find out he's been teaching me story magic? Is it my fault he's in danger?"

Grey looked her in the eyes. "Yeah."

Without further explanation, he pushed past Kaya and bolted down the dark street.

Kaya lingered there for a moment, too stunned to know what to do next. Grey had left the door open, so she peeked inside. There wasn't much there: a sleeping mat with no blanket, a table with nothing on it. Everything Grey owned had been packed inside his bag, apparently.

Hob was gone. That was what Grey had said. Hob was gone because the guild had discovered he'd been teaching his sister magic. But gone where?

He wouldn't have gone far. Not without her. Kaya needed to return home. He'd probably be there waiting for her, wondering why she'd decided to venture outside on her own so late at night.

The shortest route from Grey's place to hers would have led her through some areas best avoided by a young girl at night— or by anyone at any time of day, really. She took the long route. It was still darker and lonelier than she would have liked. If Hob had been there, she would have felt safe, but he wasn't there. That was the problem, a problem Kaya had caused by using magic.

—

As Kaya approached her home, she saw two men on their way out. They could have been there on business with the landlord, but Kaya suspected otherwise. Their fancy green uniforms marked them as guildsmen—not just apprentices, but full-fledged magicians—with the money and titles to match. The landlord usually dealt with a shadier clientele.

These men were here for Hob—or for Kaya.

If word of her public story had reached them, they'd have more than enough reason to seize her. But they could only do that if they saw her. Staying several paces from the apartment, she hid in the shadows until they left.

When she was sure the magicians were gone and not coming back, she entered the apartment. The table was knocked over, and one of the chairs was broken. Hob's sleeping mat had been torn to pieces, and chunks of the floor had been removed. Whoever those two men had been, they had trashed the place. The landlord was inspecting the damage, no doubt trying to calculate how much it would cost to fix his cheap furniture.

Kaya stared at him. Her mind raced with questions, but she couldn't figure out how to start.

The landlord didn't have such difficulties. "Two men from the Story Magicians Guild were asking about your brother. Is he hiding anything in here?"

The conjuring incense. "N-no."

He snorted. "The guild clearly thought otherwise. They said they'd be back to search again, with dogs to sniff any contraband out. What has Hob been up to?"

"I don't know. Nothing. Have you seen him?"

"The magicians said they'd taken him into custody. I don't suppose you're going to be able to pay rent, are you? I'm going to have to find new tenants." He sighed heavily before leaving Kaya alone in the wrecked room.

Normally when Kaya got upset, her stomach churned, her palms grew sweaty, and her heart raced. Not this time. Instead, she grew numb. Paralyzed. She felt as if her entire body had turned to stone. It was a struggle just to move her fingers, just to think.

She would have to pay rent. Because the guild had taken Hob into custody. They were coming back soon to search the room again.

She had to be gone by then. That was what Grey had said. Hob was gone, and they should get gone too. She wasn't sure why this involved Grey, but maybe he'd earned the guild's ire by defending Hob. That was the sort of things friends did.

Kaya needed to go, but first, she needed the conjuring incense.

It was where Hob had left it, in a small hole in the wall covered by a loose wooden slat. It was a miracle the guild hadn't seen it. Surely they could have used story magic to find it? Why did they need dogs?

Kaya didn't understand, but she was grateful nonetheless.

She took the incense, along with two of her blankets, her knitting needles, some matches, and some food. It didn't seem like nearly enough, but other than the sleeping mat and a few clay containers—items that would weigh her down—she didn't own anything else.

Chapter Six

In the little time that had passed, the temperature had fallen noticeably. Before, it had been chilly, but now it was positively cold. Even with her blankets wrapped around her, Kaya couldn't stop shivering. It didn't help that she was so scrawny, without any of the insulation that a little healthy weight would offer.

She didn't know where Anny lived—they only ever talked at the market—and she wasn't sure she'd want to go there anyway. There was too much she'd have to explain, and Anny's parents might be less sympathetic than their daughter. They might turn her away. They might even turn her in.

She *did* know of a spot where some of the street children spent the night. It was an old shack, abandoned by any official owners, and it would provide a roof to keep her dry and a fire to keep her warm. Kaya didn't head there. It wasn't that she wouldn't be welcome. Any kid who needed a place to sleep could go there, and she'd been invited before, by someone who didn't know she had a brother to take care of her. But there was still the issue of having to explain herself, and she was in no state of mind to talk to others.

Besides, she needed to do something.

The guild had taken her brother into custody. That was no better than being sent to the king's prison—worse, actually, because at least the king's prisoners had the right to a trial. The guild, on the other hand, was not technically part of the government, which meant it didn't need to abide by court laws.

If she turned herself in, would they let him go?

No. He had taught her magic. He had given her incense. In their eyes, he was just as guilty as she was. Turning herself in would only doom them both.

She needed to find her brother. He was probably imprisoned in the guildhall, located on the edge of town near the conjuring herb fields. It was a big place though, and she'd never been there before. She wouldn't know where to look for Hob. Worse yet, the place would be full of magicians, none of whom would just hand him over to her.

She had an idea. Unfortunately, it would require story magic.

She still wasn't convinced that Hob had been wrong, that the listeners punished girls who did magic with bad luck. Maybe her burned loaf had been punishment, as had Hob's trouble with the guild. Or maybe the bread had burned because she'd been careless enough to lose track of time, and the guild had seized Hob because they'd found out about the spell she'd done at the market.

Either way, it was her fault. Either way, magic was the only remaining option.

If bad luck had played a role in what had happened, another story could lead to more bad luck. She didn't see how Hob's situation could get worse, though, so if the listeners chose to punish her next story, they'd have to punish *her*. To help her brother, it was a risk she was willing to take.

She knew just the tale to tell.

—

The Story Magicians Guild controlled a large area to the west and north of Verdan. Their fields stretched for acres and acres, but Kaya didn't see the point in searching for her brother there. If the guild had him in custody, they'd have taken him to the guildhall.

It was not a place where girls were allowed to go.

She'd have to go anyway, but maybe she wouldn't have to be seen. She walked as close to the guildhall as she dared, through the dark and empty streets, past the sleepy houses, and to the edge of town.

Hidden under the cover of a tree, she lit a stick of incense. Mere moments later, a faint tingling told her it had worked.

"Listeners," she whispered, "I have a story that may interest you. There once lived a girl named Kara. If not for her brother, Hop, she would have been all alone, and she would have deserved it. She wasn't an evil girl, but she was thoughtless. She often made masks, which she thought she could sell in the market. The masks were hideous, though, and no one wanted to buy them. She kept making them anyway, wasting her few precious coins on the supplies for them.

"She grew frustrated that no one would buy her ugly masks, so she asked Hop to try one on for her. He had no desire to wear the atrocious things, but he wanted to make his sister happy, so he put one on. When she seemed satisfied, he tried to take it off, but he couldn't remove it. Kara, in her carelessness, had left a sticky paste on the inside, and now the mask was stuck to Hop's face."

Footsteps interrupted the tale. Kaya paused as a man neared. His clothes marked him as a magician—no surprise in this area. He didn't turn his head or give any other sign of noticing her presence. If he smelled the incense, he must have thought nothing of it so close to the guildhall.

Kaya held her breath as he passed.

When he was gone, she continued. "No matter how hard they tried, the mask would not budge. Before, Hop had been handsome, but now, women turned to look away from him, and small children wailed at the sight of him. He wanted to leave his town so no one would have to look at him, but Kara begged him to stay. She needed him. She asked what would make him stay. 'Hide me,' he said, and from then on, he was hidden from everyone except Kara, who took care of him the way he had always taken care of her, and he forgave her for all the damage she had caused."

Kaya hoped the story was understandable despite her chattering teeth. She wondered whether she should have created a story that would keep her hidden *and* warm, but a double spell like that took more talent and training than she possessed.

"Hide me," she said.

It worked. It worked even better than she had imagined.

Looking down, she saw only the ground, not her feet, not herself. Her belongings had vanished, along with her body. She wasn't just hidden—she was invisible.

"Thank you," she whispered. Hob had never taught her that it was necessary to do so, but it felt right nevertheless. The back of her neck tingled pleasantly for a moment, the last indication of the listener's presence before it left.

Now that the guild magicians couldn't see Kaya, it would be hard for them to find her. Unless her invisibility stopped abruptly. Or they used a spell that didn't rely upon sight to locate her. Other problems could arise too. Someone could bump into her. That would lead to a great many questions, given her invisible state. But at least now she stood a chance.

—

The guildhall was a massive building, much bigger than anything else in Verdan. Three stories tall, its height rivaled that of even the oldest trees around. Kaya was amazed it didn't collapse under its own weight, and she wondered how such a large structure could have been built. A great deal of magic must have been needed to sustain it, she imagined.

Walking carefully so her steps produced no sound, she tiptoed to the enormous door.

It was closed. Even if it wasn't locked, she feared it might be too heavy for her to open. Besides, a door that seemed to open on its own would attract attention.

She decided to wait.

The chill was worse now that she wasn't walking. Her teeth chattered, making a sound that anyone close enough could hear.

If she froze to death, no one would see her dead body, not until the spell wore off. That wouldn't happen, though, not tonight. The air was cold enough to be mighty uncomfortable, but winter was still a couple of months off.

If she didn't find her brother, she'd be spending that winter alone and on the streets. Then freezing to death would be a real concern.

A man approached. He might have been the same man who'd passed during Kaya's spell. In the darkness, she couldn't tell. It didn't matter.

He opened the door. Kaya slipped in behind him.

The inside was as impressive as the outside. The ceiling was impossibly high, though for what purpose, Kaya couldn't fathom. She couldn't help thinking the guildhall had been designed for giants.

Paintings of men lined the walls. There were at least thirty portraits, and each man looked as old, rich, and stern as the last. Kaya only recognized the most recent by name: Keen Im'Trif, the grand magician who ruled over the guild from Prima. The other men must have been previous grand magicians.

An urge grew inside Kaya. She wanted to tear the canvas, then rip the smug expressions from the grand magicians' faces. The guild had taken her brother, and she wanted them to pay. But such a petty act would achieve nothing except her own capture. She tiptoed on.

Other than the man Kaya had followed, the room was empty. He walked to the other end of the room, where there was a smaller door.

Kaya had fallen behind, and she couldn't catch up in time to make it through the door with the man. It closed in front of her, leaving her alone. Men's voices drifted through the wood, loud enough for Kaya to hear through the door.

She debated waiting for the next person, but the door was just small enough that she might have a hard time squeezing through at the same time as someone else without being noticed. She'd have to go alone.

Or she could explore another room. There was another door, on the opposite of the room she stood in. Perhaps it would lead to her brother.

Perhaps not. She could wander the large building for hours and never find her brother. But what had happened to him must have been big news around the guild. Surely some of the men would be talking about it. They might say something that would help her.

She steeled herself and pushed the door open, slowly, just a few inches. She peeked inside the noisy room. No one was looking at the door—they were too distracted to notice—so she entered.

Men sat at tables. Some of them were younger, apprentices like Hob, but most were older, full magicians. They drank and spoke and laughed, apparently unbothered by what had happened to one of their own.

She crept around them, listening.

"The wife'll be angry if I don't get home soon," one man said.

"Let her get mad," the man next to him responded. "What can she do?"

"Stop cooking for me!"

"If my wife did that, I'd turn her out on the streets."

"Yes, but your wife's a better cook than mine. Maybe just one more drink."

Kaya didn't think she'd get any good information from this table. She moved on.

"I'm surprised the listeners didn't flay you for that tale," a young man laughed, slapping his friend on the back. "That story didn't make a lick of sense."

"You just don't understand my brilliance," the young man's friend said. "Clearly the listeners do. They gave magic to my words. A lot of magicians can't say that these days."

"They probably just did it to get you to shut up."

A lot of magicians can't say that these days. Kaya didn't understand. Were the listeners flaying magicians for bad tales? That was what the other magician had expected to happen.

Whatever he meant, it had nothing to do with Hob. Kaya eavesdropped on a few more conversations. She heard the magicians brag about their girlfriends and complain about their wives. She listened to them as they told jokes and talked about their days. Sometimes they mentioned story magic, but no one said anything about Hob.

The invisibility spell might not last much longer.

"Where's Hob A'Dor?" Kaya asked, in the deepest voice she could muster. She couldn't pass as a grown man, but maybe someone would mistake her voice for that of a young apprentice.

The magicians seated next to her looked up.

"Hob?" asked one. "Isn't he on the way to Prima?"

"That's what I heard," another said. "Do you know what he did?"

The other magician shook his head. "Ace Im'Ref isn't saying. It must have been bad, though, for the guild to haul him all the way to the capital. Do you think he could have . . . ?"

Kaya wanted to stay and listen, in case they said anything else important, but she supposed she had enough information. She already knew what Hob had done. Now she knew where he was.

Besides, she had a more pressing problem at the moment. Her left pointer finger had become visible, just for a moment, before disappearing again. The spell was wearing off. She had to leave—fast.

Chapter Seven

As Kaya hurried from the guildhall, a breeze blew her hair in front of her eyes—and she saw it. She also saw her fingers, but not her arms; her shoes, but not her legs. Each second she stared, more of her form came into view. The spell was wearing off.

A half-invisible girl was more conspicuous than a fully visible girl, even if that fully visible girl was wanted by the guild. Kaya needed to hide.

Thankful for the darkness of night, she ran, putting as much distance between herself and the guildhall as she could. When she was certain she was far enough away that her presence would not arouse suspicion—though her partial invisibility would—she ducked behind a wall of crates.

They should have been sent back to the guild's farms to be filled with more flour to be sold in the market, but there was little grain these days. The crates were empty and unused, which was bad for the people who needed to sell and buy food to survive, but good for Kaya, who needed a place where she could rest undisturbed.

She couldn't crouch behind the crates forever, though. She had to come up with a plan.

The guild had taken Hob to Prima. Kaya had already known that they had taken her brother into custody, just as the landlord had said, but the conversation indicated that the situation was even worse than she'd realized. Instead of dealing with Hob in Verdan, the guild was taking him to their headquarters in Prima—which indicated that his offense had been serious.

Few ever returned after being taken prisoner by the guild. For an orphan with no connections, the chances were even worse. But Hob wasn't completely alone. He had a sister, and she was determined to save him.

—

The first step to rescuing Hob was getting out of town.

The invisibility spell finished fading about the same time the sun peeked above the horizon. With her blankets pulled over her head like a hood, Kaya ventured out of her hiding place.

She'd worried that people would spot her immediately. The guild might have been searching for her, and the boys from the market could have warned people about the girl who brought bad luck to the town by doing magic. No one said anything, though. Hardly anyone even looked at her.

Which made sense. Maybe the guild really was searching for her—or maybe not—but the average person on the street never paid her much attention, and there was no reason to expect a sudden change.

Truly, if she wanted others to ignore her, she should go back to trying to sell her blankets. People always avoided her when she was hawking her wares, asking them to part with their hard-earned coins. The louder she got, the harder people tried to pretend she wasn't there.

Kaya reached the eastern edge of Verdan without attracting any attention. Then she stepped into the wild lands that lay beyond the town.

—

By the time the late afternoon sun cast long shadows across the forest, Kaya already had two problems. One, her feet were sore. Two, her meager food supply was already dwindling.

Both things worried her, but neither came as a surprise.

Her feet had grown too large for her boots months ago. She'd hidden the fact from Hob, who would have scraped together enough money for a new pair even if it had meant borrowing from someone in the Shadows. In hindsight, that had probably been a mistake. Properly fitting shoes would have made the trek through the woods significantly less unpleasant.

Listeners couldn't make new boots materialize, but could they make existing boots bigger? Could they fix the soles, which were worn to transparency in spots?

Despite the tingling presence of a listener, Kaya decided not to find out. Even though her invisibility spell had worked, and with no consequences that she knew of, magic still carried risks. If the listeners didn't like her stories, they'd punish her. That magician in the guildhall had mentioned something about people being flayed for bad stories. Each attempt put Kaya in danger. It was best to tell stories only when absolutely necessary.

She'd need to put more thought into her tales too. So far, the listeners had overlooked her clumsy phrasing and halting narratives, but to hold their interest, she would have to become a master storyteller. She doubted she'd ever be as good as Hob, but maybe she'd be good enough.

She had a long journey ahead of her.

Although Kaya was walking east, Prima did not lie to the east. The capital city was north of Verdan, and the most direct route there would have taken her past the guildhall and through the guild's conjuring herb fields. That was why she hadn't taken it. She'd wanted to avoid the area to the west of Verdan, as well, because that was where the guild grew grain.

She couldn't walk east forever, though. She turned north.

She didn't realize her mistake until she reached the lake. She'd been so focused on avoiding the guild that she'd forgotten about the large body of water in her way.

Going around the lake wasn't an option, and not only because of its massive size. To the west, wealthy residents of Verdan had built large estates. A poor girl in a dirty dress could not wander there unbothered, whether or not the guild was looking for her. To the east, a river raged, and the only bridge for miles was watched by the king's guards, who questioned everyone who crossed.

She could swim, thanks to lessons from her brother, but not that far. And even if she could, the water would destroy the incense and matches in her pocket. Then she'd have to risk the rest of the journey alone, truly and completely alone, without the assurance that a listener could always be summoned.

She should have gone west and then north, around the guild's grain fields, not east and then north. Now she'd have to backtrack, which would waste an entire day.

But there was no other choice.

Unless she stole a boat.

One sat on the shore of the lake, secured to a post with a rope.

Kaya wasn't a thief. She'd never stolen a thing in her life, not even that one time she'd been painfully hungry and a well-off lady had left her fancy cheeses unattended on a bench. Kaya had yelled to get the lady's attention. She hadn't stolen the cheese then.

She couldn't steal a boat now.

But what about borrowing one?

Chapter Eight

Kaya only needed the boat for one short trip. It was still stealing, she knew, but this was an emergency. She approached the boat.

It was a small vessel, only large enough to sit two people. It didn't have any sails, which was fine with Kaya, who wouldn't have known how to use them anyway. She untied the rope.

"What are you doing?" yelled an old man, partially hidden by the long shadows of evening. Hobbling on a cane, he hurried toward Kaya. "Get away from my canoe!"

"Please, I just need to borrow it for a little while."

"You rotten children think you can take whatever you want!" His already quite large nostrils flared, and his bald head quivered with anger. "You'll have a hard time taking my canoe, though. Somebody already stole the paddles. Ha!"

Oh. Kaya hadn't noticed, but now that she looked at the boat, she saw that it was true. There were neither sails nor paddles. "So you can't use it?"

"Not until I make some new paddles, no. And you can't, either!"

"Do you mind if I try?" She didn't know much about canoeing, but she felt the tingling presence of a listener—and not for the first time that day. The listeners had been around, not always, but often, ever since she'd started telling tales. She was beginning to wonder if they followed story magicians around.

Which made her wonder why the guild valued conjuring herb so highly. Maybe the listeners didn't follow all storytellers—though why they would favor her, she couldn't imagine. Either she was doing something right, or the guild was doing something wrong. Both ideas seemed preposterous.

"Go ahead and try!" the old man said. "I could use some entertainment." He sat down on a tree stump, where he would get a good view of Kaya's attempts.

Kaya wasn't sure what to do with the rope—and she wasn't about to make herself look like more of a fool by asking—so she wound it into a loop and carried it with her. The boat wobbled as she stepped inside. The old man howled gleefully as she nearly fell, but she regained her balance and sat down.

"Listeners, I have a story that may interest you."

"What are you doing?" the old man yelled. "You just going to sit there?"

Kaya ignored him. He was too far away to hear—if she spoke in a low voice, which she did.

So far, all her stories had centered around a girl like herself. Such characters were easy for her, but were they boring for the listeners? Hob had used animal characters before, angry blood wolves and cursed oxen that rampaged through towns. Maybe she could do something similar.

"Once, there lived a family of caterpillars," she said, instantly regretting it. Did caterpillars even live in families? She'd never seen more than one at a time. This was why she normally stuck with characters more like herself. Regardless, she'd have to continue before the listener grew bored.

"The youngest caterpillar was very happy munching on leaves, and it never wanted things to change. But one day, things did change. Its brothers and sisters wrapped themselves in a strange white material that they called cocoons.

"The youngest caterpillar was afraid of the cocoons, and it refused to make one. Instead, it continued munching on leaves, day after day, waiting for its brothers and sisters to emerge. Finally, it happened. The cocoons opened! But the caterpillar did not recognize the strange winged creatures that emerged. They flew off, leaving the caterpillar behind.

"The caterpillar was very lonely. It was also running out of food. The air was getting cold, and the once abundant leaves had died.

"The caterpillar crawled in the direction that the winged creatures had flown. Soon, it reached a river and could go no farther. On the other side of the river, it saw the winged creatures, and it recognized them as its brothers and sisters. They were changed, but they were still family. There was food too.

"A bird landed next to the caterpillar. It had wings too. 'Take me to the other side,' the caterpillar begged the bird. The bird agreed, and so the caterpillar was reunited with its brothers and sisters."

The old man was still laughing. He didn't know she was doing story magic. Girls weren't supposed to know how, so it made sense he wouldn't suspect. To be safe, she whispered her magic words: "Take me to the other side. Please."

The boat started moving.

The man stopped laughing.

"Thank you!" Kaya shouted to him. "I'll tie it to a post or a tree on the other side for you."

The man yelled an angry reply, but soon his voice was too distant to hear. The boat was moving fast, much faster than she could have paddled. It wasn't a smooth ride. Worried that she might get knocked overboard, she sat in the center, her arms and legs tucked in. The old man disappeared in the growing distance.

The boat slowed as it approached the other side. Half on the sand and half still in the water, it stopped. Kaya got out and, a little uneasy on her feet from the bumpy ride, stepped onto the shore.

It might be days, weeks even, before the old man managed to retrieve it. Kaya felt bad about that, but all she could do was tie it to something and hope the old man got to it before the thieves did.

She was looking for a suitable tree when the boat started moving.

Kaya chased after it, but she was too late. The rope slipped through her grasp. The boat was speeding across the lake.

Speeding, not drifting. It was returning to the old man.

This hadn't been part of the spell, but the listener was doing it for her anyway.

"Thank you," she said, confused.

Something glimmered in the water under the boat. For a second, Kaya thought it must be the listener, but that was silly, of course. Listeners didn't have a physical form. They didn't do favors, either, not without a story and some carefully chosen words.

At least, that was what she'd always been taught. She could ask Hob later. But first, she had to rescue him.

—

Evening turned to night. Kaya wanted to push forward, despite her tired legs and sore feet, but the pitch blackness meant she stumbled more than she walked. The journey to Prima would take many days. She'd have to rest at some point.

The ground would have to do. She found a spot hidden by a copse of trees and softened by their fallen leaves. Wrapping her blankets around her, she lay down.

The night seemed colder now that she wasn't moving. A story could warm her blankets, if she could come up with one that was good enough. Maybe not one with animals this time.

She was still trying to think of the perfect story when she drifted off.

—

Kaya awoke to the sound of someone screaming.

It was early morning, and a sweet aroma scented the air. She hadn't noticed the smell the night before, but now it frightened her even more than the screaming. She recognized that smell. It was the unmistakable scent of conjuring herb.

She thought she'd gone far enough east to avoid the guild's territory, but perhaps she'd been wrong. The strong smell meant that the guild's fields, where they grew conjuring herb, must have been nearby—which meant the guild members themselves were also nearby.

The man yelled for help and screamed in pain. Sometimes a shrill whistle replaced the other sounds. Then the yelling and screaming resumed.

Was he a magician?

Whoever he was, he sounded desperate. He was probably hurt. Alone, too, or else he wouldn't have been yelling for help.

If she'd heard screaming like that in Verdan, she would have run to the man's aid immediately. As it was, however, she hesitated.

Which was silly, she scolded herself. Did she think it was a trap, all the way out here where the guild had no reason to expect her? Was she afraid of the stranger, even though he was injured and alone? At the very least, she could walk closer to learn what had happened.

The screams grew louder as the trees thinned. The man was close, but she could not see him.

Then she noticed the hole.

It didn't look natural; someone must have dug it. Kaya peered inside. The screaming man crouched at the bottom. He was wearing the green tunic of a guild apprentice. His arm, currently stretched upward for help, was not decorated by MAGE's blue yarn.

Several large spikes jutted out of the ground. If the man had fallen on one of those, he would have been skewered. The lack of blood—and the fact that he still breathed—indicated that he had not.

"Hurry!" the man yelled—although he was actually more of a boy, older than Kaya but younger than Hob. "Before the hounds come."

Kaya glanced over her shoulder. She didn't see any animals. "Why are you worried about dogs?"

"They're not regular dogs. The hounds are evil, and they're attracted to the conjuring herb. That's why we have these pits near the fields. To try to trap them. And I really don't want to get trapped *with* one. Are you going to help me out now?"

Of course she would.

But not immediately. She wanted more information, and she was in a position to demand it. "Why are the hounds attracted to the herb? I thought it only attracted listeners. And what do you mean, they're 'evil'? They're just animals, right?" Animals could be dangerous, Kaya knew, but they weren't evil.

"I told you: they're not regular dogs. They've got power, like the listeners. I don't know anything else. And if the guild knows, they're not telling a new apprentice like me. But believe me, you don't want to mess with those beasts."

Like the listeners? It didn't make sense. Nothing was like the listeners.

Kaya suspected this boy was lying to her, although she couldn't begin to guess his motivation. She was bothered by something else too.

"You know story magic, right?" Kaya asked, because even new apprentices knew a little. "Why do you need my help? Can't you summon a listener?"

"I told you: the herb attracts hounds too. If I burn incense, one of the hounds might come before a listener does, and that's assuming a listener comes at all. They don't like this area much, and they like the guild members here even less—not that I can blame them. Only an idiot would burn incense in hound territory. I have a whistle." He blew it, creating the shrill sound Kaya had heard before. "But none of the other guild members are close enough to hear it. Come on. My arm hurts."

"One moment," Kaya said, glad to hear that the rest of the guild was far away. That meant it was safe to ask the questions she really needed answers to. "Have you heard anything about Hob? Hob A'Dor? He's an apprentice—"

"I know who he is," the apprentice interrupted. "Why?"

"I'm his sister—" She caught herself and quickly continued. "—er's friend. His sister is very worried about him. If you could tell me something to tell her, I'd be happy to help you out."

He narrowed his eyes at her. "I don't think she'll be happy to hear what's happened. The guild is taking him to Prima for questioning. Apparently, the grand magician wants to question him personally before his execution."

Kaya's stomach twisted as her legs went weak. "Execution?" Technically, the guild had no authority to execute anyone, just as they had no right to imprison anyone. The king, however, found it easier to look the other way than to challenge the powerful magicians. Hob had often criticized the corruption. Now he would be a victim of it.

"Yeah, it's set for the twenty-ninth of Harkia. No—that's the day of the grand magician's wedding. The execution will be the next day. I hear it's going to be a real spectacle. Wish I could see it."

Rage overcame Kaya, and she was ready to leave the boy in the pit—until she realized he was calling the *wedding* a spectacle he wanted to see, not the *execution*. "The execution will be on the thirtieth of Harkia?" she asked.

The apprentice nodded.

"What day is it today?" she asked.

"The fifteenth of Harkia."

That left Kaya with fifteen days—no time to waste.

"Come on. Help me out."

Kaya reached down to pull him up. When he tried to grab hold of her hands, he yelped. "It's my arm," he explained. "I hurt it when I fell."

They tried again, but this time Kaya took hold of his one good arm. She tried to heft him up and almost fell into the pit herself, where the stakes waited to impale her.

"Give me one of those stakes," she said.

He raised an eyebrow but pulled out a stake and lifted it up to her. She shoved it into the ground near the pit. Holding on to it with one hand, she reached out for him with the other. That way, she wouldn't fall in.

His tight grasp threatened to break her fingers. Her arm ached at the stress of his weight. Slowly, though, he scaled the wall of the pit.

"Thanks. My name's Shaw. I'm pretty lucky you happened by. What brings you out here?"

"I'm traveling," Kaya said, without offering her own name.

Nodding slowly, Shaw looked her up and down. "And you're friends with Hob's sister?"

"That's right. I have to go." She started walking.

"Verdan's that way." Shaw pointed in the opposite direction. "Don't you need to talk to Hob's sister?"

"Oh. Uh, you were right—you know, what you said about her not being happy with what you had to say. You were right about that. I don't think I want to tell her."

"So where are you going?" he asked.

She didn't want to tell him she was going to Prima—he already seemed suspicious—but she didn't know what else lay in that direction. She gestured vaguely toward the north.

As she walked away, she heard him warn her, "Look out for hounds."

Chapter Nine

Kaya was more worried about starvation than evil dogs. She found some fruit and nuts to eat, but not enough to keep her stomach from grumbling. Eventually, she'd have to tell a story to get a decent meal.

But not yet. The scent of conjuring herb still perfumed the air. The guild's fields were nearby. If one of the magicians heard her doing story magic, he wouldn't need to know she was Hob's sister to have a reason to seize her. Starvation worried her more than the dogs, but the guild worried her more than starvation.

She walked as quickly and silently as she could manage.

Leaves crunched behind her.

Was it a magician? She didn't know who else would have reason to be in the area. Hoping she hadn't already been seen, she ducked behind a tree.

A deer ran past her.

Kaya laughed with relief. It was only an animal.

The relief was short lived, though. More leaves crunched. The deer had been running from something. A moment later, she saw what.

A hound.

About fifty pounds, with pointy ears and brownish-black fur, the hound could almost have passed for one of the dogs that shepherds used to manage their flocks. But no reasonable person would let this creature near livestock. Its growl made Kaya's flesh crawl. Its snarl promised violence.

A menacing red light flickered in its eyes, which were staring straight at Kaya.

Her skin tingled, but not the way it normally did when a listener lurked nearby. This was painful. Her flesh stung as if being stabbed by a thousand tiny knives.

Another hound approached, then another. An entire pack was surrounding Kaya, leaving her with nowhere to flee.

Except the trees. She grabbed a knot on the trunk that made a decent handle and scrambled up. Her foot slipped. The rough bark on the trunk tore at her boots, making the holes bigger and scratching the exposed skin. She tried again. This time, she managed to pull herself up to the lowest branch. The hounds jumped, snapping at her legs as she set her sights on the next branch.

Once she was out of the hounds' reach, she allowed herself a deep breath. The feeling of relief didn't last long. She couldn't stay up there forever.

A strong gust shook the tree. She clung to the branches to avoid falling. The hounds waited eagerly beneath her.

A twig struck Kaya's cheek. Around her, the air became thick with leaves and dirt, and wind rocked the tree back and forth—but only the one tree. The rest of the forest remained unaffected by the sudden squall.

The stinging sensation worsened. She might have clawed at her skin if she weren't so focused on hanging on.

The pain, the wind, the hounds—all of it seemed connected. But how?

Something about their red eyes suggested a supernatural force. An evil one, at that. That was what the apprentice, Shaw, had said. The hounds were like the listeners, but evil.

She searched her pockets for anything that could be used as a weapon. She had her matches. A fire might scare off the animals, but she didn't like the idea of being trapped in a burning tree.

Her knitting needles had a bit of a point to them. She threw one like a spear.

A blast of wind blew it off course. It stuck in some dirt far from her target. She lobbed the other needle, which landed in a bush several paces away.

She could think of only one thing that might help: the incense in her pocket. Shaw had said that only an idiot would burn conjuring incense in hound territory. Perhaps it didn't matter anymore. He'd been worried about attracting hounds, and the hounds were already there. Could there be more in the area, though? The last thing Kaya wanted was to attract an even larger pack.

If a listener happened to be nearby, she wouldn't need to risk burning incense. Shaw said the listeners didn't like hound territory, but maybe one would be around. She tried to sense the familiar presence, but if the tingling was there, it was drowned out by the stinging. Still, the listeners had been around a lot recently, and conjuring herb clogged the air.

A story might or might not help, but it beat doing nothing.

"Listeners, I have a story that may interest you."

Another gust of wind nearly threw her from her perch.

"It's a good one, I promise," she said, clinging to the branches for dear life. "There once lived a girl with an amazing power. She could take mud and shape it into dolls, but that wasn't the impressive part. With a kiss, the mud dolls came to life."

A branch struck Kaya's cheek, turning her words into screams.

She wiped the blood from her face and continued. "The girl made many of these dolls. Because she had created them, they did whatever she commanded. If she told them to cook dinner, they did so. If she told them to clean, they did that too."

The branch Kaya clung to creaked. Normally, it could have supported her slight weight without a problem, but the magical wind gusts were pushing the wood to its limit. Kaya looked for a sturdier branch and found none.

Speaking quickly, she said, "Unfortunately, the mud dolls were not very intelligent. When she told them to cook dinner, they baked rocks for her meal. When she told them to find firewood, they tore apart the door and used it as kindling. On top of this, they left a trail of mud wherever they went. Cleaning up after them became too much work. Although it pained her to give up on her creations, she gave them one last instruction. 'Leave,' she said, and she never saw them again."

Story magic could summon birds and oxen. Kaya hoped it could repel hounds too.

"Leave," she said.

In the trees ahead, a bird squawked. The hounds chased after the noise.

Was that the spell or only a coincidence? Unsure, Kaya jumped down from the branches. Then she ran.

Chapter Ten

Kaya ran until her chest burned, and then she kept running.

The sweet scent of conjuring herb had faded from the air. Either that, or Kaya had grown so used to it that it didn't register anymore, but she suspected the former. She slowed down to a fast walk.

The hounds and the guild weren't her only reasons for hurrying. Her brother's execution would take place in fifteen days—unless she stopped it. To do that, she had to reach Prima.

She'd heard it took about two and a half days of travel to go from Verdan to Prima, but that was for someone traveling by horse on the well-kept roads. Kaya was stomping through the woods. It would take her much longer.

And then she'd still have to locate Hob and free him. She didn't feel strong enough to do that, but she knew she had to find a way.

She wondered whether her aunt, who lived in Prima, could help.

Kaya knew very little about her ma's sister. Her name was Fiola. She had a husband. There had been a falling out between the two sisters, or maybe it was between their husbands, Kaya's pa and uncle.

Kaya didn't expect her aunt to defy the guild on her behalf, but maybe she could provide some food and a place to sleep while Kaya planned the rescue on her own.

But that was a problem for another day. Today, she walked, occasionally checking over her shoulder for hounds.

—

The night was clear, thank goodness. Kaya had tried to travel in a straight line all day, but the forest made that difficult. Every time a fallen tree or thick briar required a detour, she worried that she'd strayed too far. Now the North Star assured her she was going in the right direction. As long as she kept the bright star in sight, she knew she was headed toward Prima.

Unfortunately, while nightfall had made her general path clear, it did not help with her individual steps. Kaya was already exhausted and hungry, and the darkness proved too much. She kept tripping. After several stumbles, she did not bother to get up. Sleep took over.

—

A man's voice pulled Kaya from her dreams. She opened her eyes.

Day had broken, enabling her to see clearly, but her glances around the forest revealed no one.

If the guild had found her, they wouldn't be hiding behind trees. They'd seize her at once. But they had not done that, so they must not have found her. The voice she'd heard had probably been a product of her imagination, the last of the bad dreams that had plagued her sleep.

"Hello?" Kaya said, just to be sure she was alone. "Is anyone there?"

No one answered.

Kaya's neck tingled. It was not the painful stabbing she'd felt when surrounded by the hounds, but the pleasant tickle she'd learned to associate with the listeners. Happy for their company, she smiled.

Her stomach rumbled. It was time for breakfast, and she'd been working on the perfect story.

"Listeners," she said, "I have a story that may interest you. Once, there was a young girl given a large task: she had to feed her entire village. While the rest of the villagers sang songs and danced, she prepared countless feasts. The other villagers did not thank her for her work—not at all. Instead, they scolded her for taking too long.

"The girl did not mind. She liked working the land, as grueling as it was. She awoke each day at dawn, and she did not go to bed until long after the sun had set. Eventually, her hard work paid off. The crop of rustberries was nearly ready. She went to bed with a smile on her face, eager for the harvest the next day.

"But when she went to the field, her heart broke. There would be no pie, no jam, no bowls of fresh berries. A flock of gray crows had eaten the rustberries during the night. The last of the birds flew off as she ran onto the field.

"She searched the bushes in case the gray crows had not eaten everything, but after hours of searching, she had found only a single berry. She held it in her hand and cried. It would not be enough to feed the village. 'Grow, food, grow,' she pleaded.

"To her amazement, the berry grew. She soon struggled to hold it, and still it grew. She put it down, then stepped back to give it room. It became larger than she was, then larger than a house, and still it kept growing. When it finally stopped, she cut off pieces to make pie and jam, and the village had never been so well fed."

Kaya didn't see anything edible around—no trees with fruit or nuts anywhere—and all of summer's rustberries were long gone, but hopefully there was something she didn't see. "Grow, food, grow!" she said.

Mushrooms sprang from the ground. Kaya plucked some and popped them into her mouth. They were savory, almost meaty, though Kaya would have preferred real meat. Later, she'd work out a spell for that. In the meantime, still sitting on the forest floor, she contented herself with the bounty of fungus.

So focused on eating, she didn't notice the approaching footsteps until two figures loomed above her.

"Look at all them mushrooms," said the old man in a scratchy voice. His head was bald, his face was wrinkled, and his hands were dotted with liver spots. "Mind if we have a few?"

"Why would she mind?" said the equally old woman. Her hair was thin but long and as white as fresh snow. "She can always just magic up some more."

"I don't know what you're talking about," Kaya said. "I just found these mushrooms."

"Then you won't care if we take some," the woman said, and she and the man stuffed their pockets full. "But there's no need to deny the story. We heard you tell it. Quite entertaining, it was."

"Thank you," Kaya said automatically. "I mean, I didn't—"

"What are you doing out here?" the man asked. "Nobody good prowls this part of the woods."

"We're here," the woman said, and they both laughed.

"I'm traveling," Kaya said, getting up. "I need to be on my way."

"We could use some magic," the woman said. "We've got a—"

"I have to go," Kaya interrupted. She stepped back.

"We just need a moment of your time," the man said. "Back at our house—"

"I can't," Kaya said. She didn't know what these people wanted, but she was certain she did not want to go home with them.

The woman grabbed her wrist. "Sorry, but I must insist."

Kaya yanked her arm free.

"We need her," the woman said, and the man grabbed Kaya. She tried to fight back, but old as he was, he was bigger than her, and stronger too. The woman grabbed her legs, so she couldn't kick, and they carried her through the forest.

Chapter Eleven

Kaya didn't ask where she was being taken. She suspected she already knew.

Anny had told her tales of criminals who kidnapped magicians. They kept the magicians gagged most of the time, letting them speak only when it was time for a story, one that the kidnappers demanded. If the magician started to tell the wrong tale—one that would aid his escape, for example—the kidnappers slit his throat.

Hob had confirmed the rumor, adding that the criminals were idiots. They could have learned to tell the stories themselves, he said, and saved themselves the hassle. This did not make Kaya feel any better about her current situation.

The old man and woman took Kaya to a small shack in the woods. The woman dropped Kaya's feet and opened the door.

What kind of people lived in the woods? *Nobody good.* That was what the man had said. Kaya didn't doubt it. The forest belonged to the king, and just living there was outlawed. Kaya suspected their list of crimes would be a long one.

They carried her inside.

"Ma?" a voice asked. It sounded young—too young to be the son of such an elderly couple. "Ma, is that you? I don't feel right."

Kaya squinted in the darkness of the poorly lit shack. She saw a bed, and in the bed, a small boy.

Kaya wasn't the only child these two monsters had kidnapped. The boy was only six or seven. The guild didn't take apprentices that young, so Kaya thought the couple must not have wanted him for his magic. Which left a question: what did they want him for?

The situation was more desperate than Kaya first realized. She bit the man's hand, and he dropped her. She scrambled to her feet and balled her hands into fists.

Did the thumb go inside or outside? Inside. No, outside.

She'd never been in a fight before. Everything she knew, she'd learned from Anny, who'd learned from her two older brothers. Hob had given her a few tips, too, but mostly he'd taught her to run.

Thirdhand knowledge would have to do. The thumb went outside her fingers, Kaya recalled. That way, she wouldn't break it when she threw a punch—as if she could muster enough strength to break bones.

She swung her fist at the man, who dodged easily.

"We don't want to hurt you," the woman said, grabbing Kaya from behind.

Kaya elbowed her in the stomach and ran to the bed. "Stay away from me," she told the elderly couple. "Or I'll send the listeners after you. You've seen me do magic. You know I can do it."

The elderly couple stood back.

Kaya spoke to the boy. "Come with me."

"Ma!" the boy yelled. A blanket was wrapped tight around him, exposing only a frightened face surrounded by curly hair. "Ma, what's going on?"

The poor boy must have been delirious.

"I'll help you find your ma," Kaya said. "Now get up. We need to go."

"Ma!" he cried.

"Hush, Jor," the old woman said. "We brought her here to help."

"Get up," Kaya repeated. "We need to run."

"I can't run," the boy said. "I can't even walk. My leg's hurt. Ma! What's going on?"

Kaya would have to carry him. She wouldn't be able to take him very far, but maybe she wouldn't have to. "Where is your ma?"

The boy pointed to the old woman.

Kaya didn't understand. The woman was far too old to have a son this young. "You can't be his ma," she said.

"I didn't birth him," the woman said. "But he's mine. His leg got hurt pretty bad. The normal salve's not helping none, but your magic can. That's why we brought you here. You got to help us."

Help these people? They were criminals. Kidnappers.

Or were they desperate parents? They hadn't actually hurt Kaya. They only did what they did to help their son. Kaya would have done the same, if needed, to help her brother.

Kaya looked into their eyes, and she didn't see malice. She saw fear—and love.

"I'll do what I can," Kaya promised.

Chapter Twelve

Kaya only had fourteen days to get to Prima and rescue her brother. That didn't leave any time to waste. But helping a child wouldn't take long, and it couldn't be considered a waste of time.

The old man pulled down the boy's blanket and removed a blood-stained bandage, revealing a slash of foul-smelling pus surrounded by tender skin. The boy whimpered, a pitiful sound that made Kaya ache in sympathy. Sweat dampened the boy's face, a result of the fever he must be suffering from.

"He was fixing a leak in our roof and fell," the man said. "He tried to hide the wound for days because he didn't want to worry us. You can heal him, right?"

"I'll try," Kaya said. "But aren't you worried about bad luck?"

"Why?" the woman asked. "Because you're a girl?"

Kaya nodded.

The woman gave a dismissive wave of her hand. "The guild says the listeners cruelly punish storytellers they don't like. The Silent say all magic is evil. Me? I've not seen much magic, but what little I have has always been good. I'm not afraid of it."

Kaya was sure the Silent were wrong. The listeners weren't evil. At least, they didn't *seem* evil. Their tingling presence didn't *feel* evil.

But if they weren't evil, why would they be cruel to those who told dull stories? Perhaps the guild was wrong too.

"Please," the man said. "All we're asking for is a story."

Kaya lit a stick of incense. The scent of conjuring herb filled the air, and within moments, the back of Kaya's neck tingled pleasantly. "Listeners, I have a story that may interest you. There once lived a brother and a sister. The brother took care of the sister until, one day, he disappeared. The sister was left alone and scared, and her fear only worsened when the spiders started coming. Her brother had always liked spiders and had made her promise never to kill them, but she hated the eight-legged creatures. At first, there were only a few, crawling in her bed and spinning webs next to her head. Then there were more, and more, and more.

"The sister could not stand the spiders, but she did not want to break her promise, so she was careful only to injure them. Every day, more spiders came, and she broke their legs and tossed them outside. Their injured bodies formed piles outside her home, which she was now too afraid to leave.

"One morning, after she'd dealt with more spiders than usual, she noticed a large cobweb covering much of her ceiling. It was not a normal web. It contained a message about her brother. The spiders knew where he was. They wanted her to help him.

"She hurried outside. The spiders tried to flee from her, but their crushed legs would not let them. The sister felt sick over what she had done. 'Let this heal you,' she said, before giving them a tonic that would restore their strength and heal their legs. Then the spiders led her to her brother, who had fallen into a ravine and was trapped there. The spiders made a rope out of their silk, and she used it to pull him out. The siblings lived happily ever after, and she never hurt a spider again."

Kaya looked at the boy, whose pitiful face she'd been avoiding. "Let this heal you."

The boy wept.

"What's wrong?" Kaya asked. She feared she already knew. She had angered the listener. She'd been asking for too much, and her stories weren't good enough.

It was bad luck for girls to practice story magic. It was wrong of her to try.

Still weeping, the boy smiled. "It doesn't hurt anymore."

The old woman dabbed his leg with a rag. The blood and pus wiped away, exposing healthy brown skin. "Thank you," she said, her words barely intelligible through her tears. Even the old man's eyes were moist.

"I didn't really do anything," Kaya protested. "It was the listener."

"Maybe so, but you brought the listener here, and for that we're in your debt. My name's Roya, and this here is Qir." Wiping tears from her wrinkled cheeks with one hand, she gestured to the old man with the other. "And the boy you just healed is Jor."

"I'm Kaya."

Roya nodded slowly. "Nice to meet you, Kaya. I'm sorry about the way we met. I hope you understand that we're not bad people. We just couldn't let you leave without seeing why we needed your help. Our shack isn't much, but it's better than the forest, and we could use a talented storyteller such as yourself. How would you like to stay?"

"Thank you, but I can't. I'm looking for my brother."

"Like your story. Only, I doubt any spiders will help you." Roya made a noise that sounded like a creak but might have been a sigh. "Can you at least stay for lunch? I'm going to add those mushrooms to a nice stew for us. There's meat in it." She didn't say what kind. Squirrel, maybe, or dirt-dove.

Kaya didn't care. A hot meal sounded lovely, and it would give her the energy she needed to walk the rest of the day. "Yes, that would be nice."

While Roya added mushrooms to the stew, Qir and Jor questioned Kaya about story magic.

"You must be rich," Jor said, his dark eyes wide with wonder. At the moment, he was sitting on a bench, but he was having a hard time staying still. He kept fidgeting, and every once in a while, he'd jump out of his seat. "If I could do magic, I'd make a ton of gold."

"The listeners can't make gold," Kaya said wisely. "They can heal." She pointed to Jor's leg as she said this. "And they can help things grow, but they don't actually *create* anything."

"Then I'd grow expensive fruits and herbs and stuff and sell them to all the rich people who live in town."

Kaya hadn't thought of that. It might work—or not. "There are very few rich people these days. You'd have a hard time selling luxury goods. And trying would get you noticed by the guild. They don't take too kindly to unauthorized storytellers."

"Like you," Qir said.

Kaya hesitated, but there was no point in lying. Everyone knew girls were banned from practicing magic. "Yes. Like me."

"Can you show us? That way, we could do it for ourselves."

"It's dangerous," Kaya said. "And I'm new at it myself." What if she forgot some important warning, and they suffered as a result?

"Is it true that they attack people who tell bad stories?" Jor asked, jumping up from his seat for the hundredth time.

"You know it's not," Roya said. "The listeners are good. They just healed you."

"But my brother told me about a man that asked for better eyesight," Jor insisted. "The listeners didn't like his story much—it was one they'd heard before—so they blinded him instead. Or maybe they boiled his eyes. He told it both ways."

"You have a brother?" Kaya asked.

The happy expression faded from Jor's face. "Jay. He disappeared a few months ago. He said he was going to get us a deer, but he never came back."

One of the hounds might have gotten him—or maybe a regular pack of blood wolves. "You must miss him. I know I miss my brother."

"Yeah." He looked sad for a moment, but then he smiled. "You're pretty smart to think up all those stories, huh?"

"Not that smart," Kaya mumbled, her face turning hot. "My brother's smart, and he's taught me well."

"Stop pestering our guest," Roya said. "Look how you embarrassed her!"

Roya served the stew she'd made. Kaya devoured her food in seconds.

"You must be hungry," Roya said, scooping her another serving.

"It's very good." Kaya accepted the refill and took another bite. "Do the hounds ever come around here?" she asked, thinking about Jor's missing brother.

"No, we don't got no dogs," Qir said. "Why?"

"There are hounds near the guild's fields. Not regular dogs. There's something different about them. Something dangerous." Something evil and magical, too, but Kaya kept that to herself. They wouldn't have believed her if she'd said anything. Everyone knew that only the listeners had magic. "They live in the forest near the conjuring herb fields. You should stay away."

"Well, we keep far away from them guild members," Roya said, "so I don't reckon we'll have problems with the hounds."

That was probably why nobody knew of the horrible beasts. Most people avoided the guild's fields, so they never encountered the hounds. The occasional person who did happen upon them might not live to tell the tale—like Jor's brother, if Kaya's hunch was right.

The guild knew about the hounds, of course, but they weren't big on sharing information. Kaya wondered whether

Hob knew. If so, he would have been outraged. That could have been why he'd joined MAGE.

It was one more thing she'd have to ask him—after she rescued him.

"Are you sure you don't want to stay?" Roya asked. "Just for one night, at least? It's a long way from here to any sign of civilization."

"I can't," Kaya repeated. "I should be going now. Can you show me which way is north?"

Qir pointed her in the right direction, and with a heaviness in her heart, Kaya resumed her long trek to Prima.

Chapter Thirteen

Kaya walked well into the night, but eventually she had to find a spot to sleep. The next morning, she awoke at dawn and continued walking. *Thirteen days*, she thought.

When the cold made her shiver or the thick underbrush snagged her dress, she found herself wishing she could have taken Roya up on her offer. It wasn't the food, which was good but not better than Kaya's own cooking. It wasn't the shack, which was even more run-down than her old apartment. It was the family.

For years, Hob had been the only family she'd had. He was wonderful and smart, and he kept her safe—but he was only one person. She missed the way a real family could fill a home with laughter and warmth, even if the home in question was a dilapidated shack in the middle of the woods.

Would her aunt and uncle in Prima accept her as family? She *was* family, technically, but she was also a stranger.

The only family she could count on was Hob—and she only had thirteen days to save him. Thinking about anything else was selfish. She walked on.

—

Kaya's heart filled with joy at the sight of a tree. A tree in a forest might not sound like anything special, but this one was different. It was a crabapple tree, its branches weighed down with an abundance of fruit.

"Look at these crabapples!" she said. "Have you ever seen any so beautiful?"

There was no response, of course. Kaya was alone—more or less. There were the listeners. She'd felt their tingling presence often. This gave her comfort—and not only because it meant she could do story magic without wasting a precious stick of incense. Perhaps it was just because she was so lonely, but she was starting to think of them as her traveling companions.

She'd taken to speaking to them, even when she didn't have a story to tell. She worried that it might annoy them, but they didn't seem bothered. They stuck around anyway. Besides, Hob had never warned her not to.

She commented on everything—the chill in the air, the birds in the trees, the hunger gnawing at her stomach, and the beautiful crabapple tree she'd happened upon.

"Would you like a crabapple?" she asked. "Do listeners even get hungry?"

They didn't answer, of course, but she still enjoyed talking.

Whether or not the listeners got hungry, she did. She ate two crabapples and stuffed her pockets with as many as she could fit. The fruit wasn't as filling as the stew had been, but at least it was something to put in her belly.

—

When Kaya came to a pond, her mouth watered with excitement. Fish was almost as good as meat—much better than crabapples.

She didn't have a fishing rod or net—or the experience to use them. She had some matches, for the incense, but knew little about building fires or cleaning fish.

With the right story, it wouldn't matter. This would be her most ambitious tale yet.

"Listeners," she said immediately, because the tingling was quite strong and there was no need for conjuring herb, "I have a story that may interest you. There once was a small village surrounded by lush fields, and these fields produced all the fruit, nuts, and mushrooms the villagers could eat. There were also wild goats that allowed themselves to be milked and chickens that left eggs for the villagers, and no one ever went hungry.

"Then, one year, the fruit and nut trees stopped producing, the mushrooms stopped growing, and the chickens and goats fled. The villagers had some jam and nuts left from previous years, but it was a meager supply, and it dwindled quickly. The villagers began to starve.

"Several of the elders formed a council to decide what had to be done. The council decided that there was no sense in letting everyone die. Although they had never tasted meat before, they knew it was edible. Since the goats and chickens had left, they would slaughter a human."

The tingling faded slightly. Worried that the listener was growing bored, Kaya spoke faster. "They chose an old woman who had come from another village in a faraway land and was therefore an outsider. Before they could kill her, however, she told them of another way. There was a pond, accessible only through a cave outside the village, and there were fish in the pond. 'Catch, clean, and cook the fish,' she said.

"The old woman showed the villagers how to do it, and they were grateful to have a new source of food and not to have to kill anyone."

The tingling had faded even more, so that it was now barely noticeable. But the listener was still there. "Catch, clean, and cook the fish," Kaya said.

Nothing happened.

The listeners had rejected her story.

Chapter Fourteen

Kaya couldn't be sure why the listeners had rejected her story, but she supposed they simply hadn't liked it enough. She'd been trying to work on her storytelling skills, but apparently, she hadn't been working hard enough.

Although Kaya still felt the tingling presence of the listeners sometimes, she was reluctant to try another spell. One story had been ignored. The next could be punished. Tongues had been ripped out after bad stories. Eyes had been gouged out. Men had dropped dead. Better not to risk it unless she had no other choice.

The following days blended together in a haze of tired feet and hunger pangs.

—

Kaya had been avoiding roads, lest she be seen by the guild, but when she happened across one, she was tempted to take it.

The guild might be looking for her in Verdan, but Verdan was far away now. Surely, no one was looking for her here.

The smooth road would make walking easier.

Even better, it went north. Could it lead to Prima?

She decided to find out. She ran along the road. Soon, she saw buildings up ahead.

A metal ring encircled the settlement in front of her. It was almost as if someone had marked the location of a wall but had forgotten to actually build it. Kaya knelt down to inspect the thin, hard metal.

"What do you think it is?" she asked the listeners, but only out of habit. She did not feel their tingly presence.

She hesitated. Whatever this place was, it wasn't Prima. It looked small, even smaller than Verdan—much too small to serve as the seat of both the government and the guild. And since it wasn't Prima, any time spent there would amount to a delay in her brother's rescue. Only eleven days remained until his execution.

But the town would have food, and Kaya needed to eat. She hadn't had a proper meal since Roya's stew, three days ago. She entered the town.

—

The market was not what Kaya was accustomed to. No one played music or juggled for coins. No homeless children begged for money.

There was food, though. A street vendor sold steaming chunks of meat. The aromas wafted into Kaya's nostrils and made her mouth water. If the vendor turned his back, maybe she could snag a chunk.

Before, she'd insisted to herself that she wasn't a thief. She'd only borrowed the boat; she hadn't stolen it. The distinction had seemed important to her then.

Now—weak, exhausted, and hungry—she found it increasingly difficult to care.

If she was going to steal, though, she might try for something more than a small piece of meat—something that could last her the rest of her journey.

There were several coins in easy view.

They were in a purse. The purse was hanging from a broken strap, and the broken strap dangled from the shoulder of a young woman. Aside from the frayed purse string, she was well dressed, with a pretty skirt and shirt that suggested she wouldn't miss a few coins.

Kaya grabbed them.

The woman lurched forward. She'd felt the hands tugging at her purse. She would turn around and see Kaya standing there, the stolen coins clutched in her criminal hands. The authorities would throw her in jail, where she would rot. Without anyone to help him, Hob would be executed.

No. The woman was only stepping forward to continue wherever it was she was going. She hadn't noticed anything.

Kaya looked around, her heart racing. Someone must have seen her. One couldn't just get away with crimes. Someone had seen her. Someone would report her, and she would be arrested—and justifiably so.

The woman looked well off, but that meant little. Some families upheld the appearance of prosperity long after their riches had dwindled, whether out of pride or vanity or the hope that they would recover soon. The woman might have had her fine dress and her coins and nothing else. Perhaps she had planned to invest the coins in a new venture, her family's last opportunity to regain its wealth. That was why she hadn't replaced the torn purse. She hadn't possessed the money to spare.

Kaya had stolen from her. Someone must have seen. She would be caught and turned in, and she would deserve it.

"I'm sorry!" she said to the woman, who had walked several paces ahead by now. In order to be heard, Kaya was practically yelling.

The woman stopped, as did everyone else who happened to be nearby.

"I'm sorry," Kaya repeated, holding out the stolen coins. "These are yours."

The woman took the coins. Much to Kaya's surprise, she was smiling. Her big amber eyes sparkled with joy and kind-heartedness. "Oh, they must have fallen out of my purse. Silly me, I keep meaning to buy a new one, but this is my favorite, you see. I suppose I could have it fixed, but then I'll have to drop it off and be without it for a while and—oh, listen to me babble!" She took a moment to look at Kaya, and her smile faltered. "Oh dear, look at that dress of yours. I'm surprised you didn't keep the coins for yourself. That's what most people would have done. Well, come with me. I can give you a meal and help you get cleaned up—as a reward for your honesty."

Kaya followed the woman—the offer of free food was not one she could ignore—but she didn't feel good about it. A reward for her honesty? Nothing about what Kaya had done had been honest.

She went without a word of this.

The woman led her to a house—a real, proper house quite unlike the hovel Kaya and Hob had rented. Its white paint gleamed so brightly that it was almost painful to look at, but Kaya did, anyway, because it was just that pretty.

Two large doors opened to reveal the interior of the house, which was even more beautiful than the exterior. Fine paintings decorated the walls, and plush rugs softened the wood floors. Not a single speck of dust or mold marred the elegance.

"I didn't catch your name," the woman said.

"Kaya A'—" She stopped. In case the guild was looking for her, she shouldn't give her real name. "Bon. Kaya A'Bon."

She gave a sympathetic frown. "An orphan. I should have guessed. My name is Belma S'Vale. Come inside. Sit down. I'll get some food for you."

S'Vale. The name indicated that her family belonged to the upper class. They owned land, and they may have increased their riches through other trades as well. They could have been artists, which would explain the abundance of paintings—there was more canvas than wall visible in the large sitting room.

While Belma disappeared into another room, Kaya sat uncomfortably on the sofa. The velvety cushions and pillows weren't the problem, not exactly. It was just that they were white, and Kaya's dress was more dirt than cloth at this point. Afraid of the stains she might cause, she tried not to put her weight on the expensive furniture and, as a result, ended up crouching rather than sitting.

Belma returned with a plate of sandwiches. The bread was as white and fluffy as the sofa, and it was filled with meat smothered in a creamy sauce.

Kaya ate all the sandwiches before realizing that Belma might have intended for them to share. "Sorry."

Belma laughed, and it sounded like bells ringing. "Whatever for? Do you want some more to eat?"

"No, thank you." Kaya stood, checking the cushion as she did so. Dirt smudged the white velvet. "I'm sorry. I've stained your sofa."

"Oh, don't worry. It'll be fine after a good cleaning—like you! Why don't I get a bath running for you? I don't have any clothes that will fit you, but I can wash that dress if you don't mind staying the night while it dries."

"No, I can't. Thank you, but I should be going."

"Going where? I don't think I've seen you before. Do you live here?"

"No, not here." Or anywhere, anymore. The landlord would have rented the room out to someone else by now. The few items she'd owned—the sleeping mat and the pots—would have been sold. "I'm going to Prima to res—to see my brother."

"Prima? But that's so far! Are you traveling on your own, with no carriage, no horse? Why, you're just walking through the woods!"

Kaya looked down at her worn, mud-caked boots, embarrassed. "I have to."

"Well, you can at least rest here for a night. It'll be dark soon. I'll get you that bath, and then you can have some dessert before going to bed. How does that sound?"

Wonderful, Kaya had to admit. She looked out a large, curtain-lined window. The sun was close to setting. Kaya would have to sleep somewhere. She might as well do it in a warm bed.

Kaya nodded. "Thank you."

She worried a bit about spending the night in a stranger's house, but strangers weren't all bad. Roya and her family had been kind. Belma seemed nice, too, so what harm could a decent night's rest do?

Chapter Fifteen

The bathroom was larger than Hob and Kaya's entire rented apartment had been. Clouded windows let in light while framed paintings offered decoration. The floor was marble, and the fixtures—a sink, a tub, and a toilet—were porcelain.

At first, the idea of doing her business inside disgusted her—there was a reason outhouses were outside, namely the smell—but then she saw how flowing water washed everything away.

"Is the water magic?" Kaya asked.

Belma's nose wrinkled. "Magic? No. No, of course not. It's just the pipes." She gestured to the pipes that ran under the sink and next to the bathtub. "Leave your clothes outside the door so I can have them washed. There's a robe you can wear until they're ready."

Belma left. After removing the conjuring incense, matches, and empty coin purse from her pockets, Kaya pulled off her mud-stiffened clothes, which she folded into a neat square. The robe Belma had mentioned hung on a hook on the wall, but she didn't want to dirty it by putting it on before her bath. Completely naked—and feeling very exposed—she cracked the door open and slipped the filthy clothes into the hall.

The tub was almost full now. She tested the water with a single finger and was pleasantly surprised. It wasn't cold, as she'd expected. The pipes themselves might not have relied on magic to operate, but surely a story was responsible for this wonderful warmth. She stepped into the tub and sighed with delight.

The wealthy sure had it good. If the tub were hers, she'd take baths all the time—at least once a week.

A fancy glass bottle containing a thick liquid sat next to the tub. Kaya opened it and sniffed. The scent of flowers wafted into her nostrils. She poured a little of the liquid into the water, which transformed into bubbly foam upon contact. After a few minutes, the bubbles dissipated, and she reached for the bottle again.

Her fingers were slick with water and soap.

The bottle slipped out of her grasp.

The beautiful glass shattered against the marble floor. A puddle of flower-scented soap covered the shards.

First, she'd tried to steal from Belma. Now she'd destroyed Belma's precious belongings. The bottle itself must have cost a small fortune, not the mention the soap inside.

Kaya had made a mess—but she could fix it.

Careful not to step on the broken glass, she got out of the tub and put on the robe Belma had supplied. Even in her state of distress, she couldn't help noticing how soft the material was.

She didn't feel the tingling presence of a listener, but that was only a temporary inconvenience. She lit a match and touched the flame to a stick of incense.

Nothing happened. Strange. Normally, a listener appeared almost instantly, and that was assuming she had to conjure one at all. But she supposed it was selfish of her to expect listeners to be available at her beck and call. They had other things to do, probably, although she couldn't even begin to guess what those things might be.

Maybe she just had to wait a little longer. She watched as the stick of incense turned to ash.

The door flew open. "What is that smell?" Belma asked. "Is something burning?" Belma's eyes widened. She'd spotted the broken bottle, Kaya thought, and would kick her out because of it.

But when Belma spoke next, it wasn't about the bottle. "Is that conjuring incense?" She was staring at the small pile of ash and the wooden stem, all that remained of the stick Kaya had burned.

Oh. "No, it's, uh, it's—"

"Stay here," Belma said, her face stern. She fled the bathroom, shutting the door behind her.

Kaya did as ordered. For a while. Belma was gone for a long time, though, and Kaya's anxiety grew with each second that passed. Belma had seemed nice, but what if she supported the guild? What if she was informing the guild of the incident now?

Kaya had to leave.

Her robe didn't have any pockets, but she managed to secure the matches, coin purse, and remaining incense under the thick belt, which was big enough to hide the items well. Then she headed for the door.

It wouldn't open.

The knob turned, but the door refused to budge. Something large had been placed on the other side.

When Belma had told Kaya to stay, she'd neglected to mention that Kaya would have no choice in the matter. She was trapped.

Chapter Sixteen

The listeners rarely ignored the smell of burning incense, but it was known to happen occasionally. Hopefully, a second stick would attract them. Kaya had to try. The guild would arrive soon, having been tipped off by Belma. On the bright side, Kaya might be taken to the same cell as Hob—but as a prisoner of the guild, she'd have no way to free him. No, she had to get there on her own. She had to get out of the bathroom.

The burned incense lingered in the air.

No listeners responded to the scent.

What was keeping them?

She tried the door again. Maybe it wasn't blocked. Maybe it was stuck. The wood had swollen from the moisture of the bath. No one had trapped her inside. She was being paranoid.

But the door didn't budge. It was definitely blocked. Paranoid or not, she was trapped.

There was a window. It was too thin and too high, but Kaya might manage to climb up and squeeze out. She could try, anyway.

She pushed a vanity table beneath the window. The porcelain furniture was slippery, so she had to move slowly and cautiously to avoid falling.

The door opened.

Surprised, Kaya lost her balance and tumbled to the floor.

A moment later, Belma was standing over her, flanked by two other women.

"This is the bedeviled child," Belma said. The women yanked Kaya up and dragged her away.

—

Kaya was taken to a stone building, to a large room with high ceilings but no windows, where she was told to sit in a chair located in the very center. Strange symbols had been etched into the walls. She didn't see any sign of the guild—no apprentices dressed in green tunics, no banners bearing images of broad-leafed plants—but nevertheless, she was sure the guild would be coming for her.

But the person who arrived was another woman.

She was old. A stern expression had etched itself permanently into her wrinkled face. Her gray dress matched her gray hair.

She was a woman—and therefore not a guild member—but the others acted as if she was in charge.

"You have been brought here on charges of bedevilment," she said. "Do you confess?"

Kaya shook her head. How could she confess when she didn't even understand the question?

"Villy, I saw her with the incense they use to summon the devils," Belma said. "She must have hidden it under her robe."

The old woman, Villy, quickly zeroed in on the belt, the only place where Kaya could conceal anything. Within seconds, the old woman had found the incense.

"It's not to summon devils. It's to summon listeners." And because girls weren't supposed to summon anything, Kaya added, "It's my brother's. I was holding it for him."

"Your so-called listeners *are* devils," Villy said. "Do you confess to dealing with them?"

"I was just holding it. I know girls aren't allowed—"

"We don't care that you're a girl. You have had contact with the devils. You would have summoned them here and sullied our town, if not for our sacred barrier. You must be cleansed."

—

The "cleansing" Villy had in mind was nothing like the lovely bath Kaya had taken. For one thing, there was no water, flower-scented or otherwise. Just lots and lots of yelling.

The entire town must have shown up to participate.

They were the Silent, Kaya realized, the people who thought the listeners were evil. Anny had gossiped about them, and Roya had mentioned them, as well, but Kaya had assumed their numbers must have been few. She'd never expected to stumble upon an entire town of people with such strange beliefs.

She should have headed straight to Prima, straight to Hob. Now she was trapped, while her brother's execution became closer to reality with each passing moment.

She was back in her own clothes, which were clean because Belma had had them washed before the accusations of bedevilment started, but which were also soaking wet. Her blankets, rather worse for wear and heavy with water, were wrapped around her shoulders.

Belma and the other women had dragged Kaya outside to the center of town, and they'd stopped in front of the wooden pillory. Kaya recognized it immediately, having seen a similar contraption before. Her own town had one, which was used to punish thieves and cheats.

Her head was secured in one big (though not that big) hole, while her wrists were stuck in two smaller holes. A man of average height would have had to lean forward to fit. Kaya, much shorter than a grown man, had had no choice but to stand on her tiptoes.

The townspeople shouted at her.

"Be gone, devil-user!"

"Stay out of our town!"

"Keep your evil away from us!"

Kaya kept alert for the telltale tingle of the listeners. If she could work some story magic, she could free herself from the pillory, maybe create a mist or something to hide her as she ran away.

No listeners came.

Why had they deserted her? Was it because of the sacred barrier Villy had mentioned? Kaya had never heard of such a thing, and she couldn't begin to imagine how it would work.

Nothing could stop listeners. If they wanted to help Kaya now, they would.

At least the townspeople were only yelling. The way they'd talked about devils and filth, she'd feared the cleansing might be something worse.

She'd been right to fear.

A rotten crabapple hit her shoulder.

A small rock hit her next.

Chapter Seventeen

*E*ventually, the barrage of fruit and pebbles ended, and the yelling quieted. The crowd dispersed, but Villy lingered. Some of the rocks had been large enough to leave Kaya with bruises and cuts, but none of her injuries were very severe.

Still stuck in the pillory, Kaya twisted her neck so she could look Villy in the eyes. "You did your cleansing. Now can I go?"

Villy chuckled. "The cleansing isn't over. That was only phase one. The hunger trial is next, followed by the fire purification. Only then will you be saved from the devils." She left—without releasing Kaya.

—

Night fell. The air was chilly, and Kaya's clothes were still damp. She shivered, but the cold was not her biggest concern. Rats had arrived to eat the rotten fruit that lay on the ground at Kaya's feet. Sometimes they nibbled at her feet too. She kicked them away, but they always came back. They were hungry.

So was she.

Was this the hunger trial?

If so, Kaya wasn't overly alarmed. She'd dealt with hunger before. The fire purification, on the other hand, had her much more worried. Did they intend to burn her alive? She couldn't think of what else Villy could have meant, and she wouldn't put the cruelty past these people.

Hob had less than eleven days left. How long did she have?

"Listeners," she whispered, despite not feeling their presence, "I'm really sorry if my stories haven't been good enough. But now I have a story that you may enjoy. Please. I—OW!"

A rat was biting her toe, which poked through a tear in her boot. She thrashed her foot around until the rat scampered away.

It was no use. For whatever reason, the listeners had abandoned her. She had to escape on her own—before the fire purification began.

The pillory consisted of two wooden boards placed one on top of the other. A simple latch held them together. If she could undo it, escape would be easy. That was a big *if*. Her attempt accomplished nothing except a sore shoulder. She couldn't reach the latch.

"Help!" she yelled, because maybe some of the townspeople didn't support what had happened. She only needed one person to take pity on her and let her go.

The townspeople were as absent as the listeners.

Maybe she could break the pillory. She rocked back and forth, trying to force the pillory over. She'd fall with it, but the impact might knock something loose. If she got really lucky, the latch might come undone.

Luck wasn't on her side, though. The heavy pillory refused to budge.

"Help!" she called again, to no response. "Help! Help! Help!"

Her body was shaking. Her breaths were fast and shallow. She sobbed until she passed out from exhaustion.

—

When Kaya awoke, it was still dark out. She was calmer or perhaps just groggy. Either way, she wasn't panicking anymore.

Her body ached—her shoulders and neck worst of all. She tried to stretch, the way she normally would after waking up stiff from an uncomfortable nap, but with her hands and head secured in place, there wasn't much room for that. Maybe if she squeezed her fingers and thumb together, she could pull her hands through the pillory enough to increase her range of motion.

It worked.

Better than she'd expected.

Forget about stretching. She could escape.

The pillory hadn't been made for a child, she realized. Why would it have been? Nobody made pillories for children. The pillory had been designed for adults, for grown men even, and the holes had been cut accordingly.

At twelve years old, Kaya considered herself nearly mature, but she was scrawny too. If she tried, she might manage to slip her hands through.

She pulled and tugged. When the wood scraped her hands, she bled. But she was making progress. A little more, a little more—

Success! She pulled one hand through, minus one or two layers of skin lost in the process.

Then it was time for her other hand. It was easier, though no less painful, now that she knew what to do.

She'd freed her hands. Next, she had to free her head. She tugged, twisted her neck, and tugged some more, but the hole wasn't big enough.

The latch wasn't that far away, though. Now that her hands were free, she should be able to reach it—

Another rat bit her toe. She kicked it, lost her balance, and stumbled. She would have fallen to the ground if her head hadn't been secured in place. As it was, the half-tumble wrenched her neck, and she yelped.

What time was it? Soon, the sun would rise, and the townspeople would follow.

Kaya resumed stretching. Her fingers felt the latch. She fumbled with it, unable to get a good look at it and unsure of which way to move the latch. Left? Or right? Up or down? After a little trial and error, it opened.

She pulled up the top half of the pillory. She was free.

But if the townspeople saw her, she wouldn't stay that way for long. She had to hurry.

Chapter Eighteen

Kaya did her best to head in the right direction, but the cloudy night meant she couldn't use the stars to guide her. At the moment, her biggest concern was getting away. She went in the direction she thought—hoped—was north as fast as she could.

The clouds also meant the night was darker than normal—good for slipping away unnoticed but bad for making sure one didn't trip. At least her dress and blankets had dried.

Something glinted on the ground. Kaya stooped down to examine the thin line of metal. It was identical to what she'd seen when entering the town.

Could this be what Villy had meant by a sacred barrier?

No. It didn't make sense. A line like this, no thicker than a windowpane, couldn't stop anything, much less a powerful listener. Kaya didn't know what it was for, but it wasn't that.

There was a road. It probably led to Prima, but Kaya didn't dare travel on it, not when people might be chasing after her. Nevertheless, she was happy to see it, as it reassured her that she was going in the right direction. She traveled parallel to the road, moving as fast as she could through the dense forest, eager to put as much distance as possible between herself and the town.

Although a part of her was tempted to return.

They'd taken her incense.

For most of her life, she'd had her parents and then Hob to take care of her, and then she'd had magic to help her manage, but now she had nothing at all. On her own, she felt lost. Helpless. Doomed.

But her brother needed her, so she pushed on.

After Kaya had been walking for a while, her neck tingled, just for a second. Maybe she'd imagined it, a symptom of her exhaustion. Regardless, she had no stories to tell and no breath to spare on them. She had to keep walking as fast as she could. Every once in a while, she checked over her shoulder, afraid that someone would be chasing after her, ready to drag her back for the fire purification Villy had threatened.

The sun rose, then set again before Kaya was confident no one was following her. She had lost sight of the road, but the stars confirmed that she was heading in the right direction.

She wanted to keep walking. Although she was safe now, or as safe as a girl could be wandering the forest at night, Hob had less than ten days left. She needed to hurry, but her body had other ideas. Two trees had fallen, forming a crisscross shape that provided decent coverage. Too tired to mind the bugs or the dampness, Kaya curled up and fell asleep.

—

Kaya tracked the days carefully. Each one that passed made her brother's situation that much more dire.

She ate mushrooms and nuts, as well as some half-rotted fruit. She also came across a bed of worms, which some boys back in Verdan had told her made a nutritious meal in a pinch, but she couldn't bring herself to eat the wriggling things.

She couldn't bring herself to tell a story, either, not even when she felt the listeners' tingling presence. They'd ignored her last story, and then they'd abandoned her. If she told another one they didn't care for, what would they do?

Perhaps the Silent were right after all. The listeners were cruel. They were evil.

No. She didn't believe that. The listeners' tingling presence filled her with warmth and happiness. It made her feel safe. How could anything evil do that? Although she hesitated to tell another story, she still talked to them as she walked.

A storm came, and the ground turned to mud that seeped into the ever-growing holes in Kaya's boots. Every once in a while, she stopped to remove the muck and the weight it added, but it was like trying to ladle water out of a sinking ship. Eventually, she took off her boots and carried them. Her clean clothes and blankets became filthy again.

At night, sleet replaced the rain. It stung Kaya's cheeks, but only until her face became numb.

When she awoke early the next morning, it was to the sound of growling.

It sounded like a dog. A hound, maybe. Did they live in this region? Kaya didn't have anyone to ask.

She didn't have anyone at all.

Despite her best attempts to stay still and silent, the growling came closer. The beast—hound or otherwise—was approaching.

In the darkness, Kaya couldn't see it until it was a few feet away. It wasn't a hound. It was a lone blood wolf. A young and scrawny one, hardly older than a pup, and too small to take on a human of Kaya's size—except that it was clearly very hungry, and Kaya was clearly very weak. As it watched her, Kaya felt as though she understood its dilemma. Should it pounce and risk injury? Or leave and face starvation?

Kaya jumped up and yelled.

The blood wolf ran off.

The next one might not.

—

Kaya had been walking all day. Sore, tired, and hungry, she was ready to give up. It had been foolish of her, she realized, to think she could make the trek to Prima on her own.

She collapsed on the ground and sobbed. "I can't do it!" she cried. "I'll never reach Prima."

Kaya's skin tingled.

"What do you want?" Kaya asked. "A story?"

The tingling intensified, just for a second.

Of course the listener wanted a story. That was all they ever wanted. And Kaya wanted to tell one, despite her exhaustion. Walking without the listeners' help had been hard. Lonely.

"If I tell a story and you don't like it, you'll punish me, won't you?"

Again, the tingling intensified briefly. It was an answer—but did it mean yes or no?

"Do it once if you will punish me for a bad story," Kaya said. "Twice if you won't."

The tingling intensified, then faded, intensified, then faded.

At least Kaya thought it did. She was so tired and sore that her mind could have been playing tricks on her.

She'd been walking for a long time. Too long. She should have reached Prima by now. She'd messed up, gone the wrong way or something. Hob only had seven days before his scheduled execution. If she had any chance of saving him, she needed help.

"All right, then, listeners, I have a story that may interest you. There once lived a girl who had to take a terrible test. It was a test that everyone in her city took before becoming an adult. If she failed, she'd be banished. She wanted to prepare, but no one would tell her what the test would involve, so all she could do was worry.

"On the day of her thirteenth birthday, it was time. Her ma and pa led her outside the city, through the forest, and to a small building. They told her to go inside, and even though there was no lamplight and she could not see, she did. Then she fell.

"She fell for a long time, long enough to think about what was happening. This had to be part of the test, she reasoned. Not that this would help her land, which she eventually did, with a painful thump.

"Now there were lamps—two of them, each held by a woman. One woman was young and beautiful, with gleaming hair and full lips. The other was old and wrinkled, with a wart-covered nose and a humped back. They spoke in unison, telling her that one of them would help her and the other would hurt her, and she had to choose whom to trust. She chose the young woman, certain that anyone that beautiful must be good.

"The old woman stepped aside. The young woman offered her a cup. Thirsty, the girl drank from it.

"Everything plunged into darkness. For a moment, the girl thought the lamp had gone out, but then she realized the horrible truth. The drink had blinded her. She had chosen wrong. She had failed the test. Now she would never find her way home.

"But the girl would not give up so easily. She could not see with her eyes, so instead she felt with her hands. She found a trickle of water to drink and patches of fungus to eat. She also found the old woman. The girl apologized and offered to share whatever water and food she found. The woman never accepted the food or water, but she did sit and talk with the girl. Over time, the old woman seemed to take pity on her. 'Show me the way to the city,' the girl begged, and the old woman guided her home. The girl never regained her sight, but because she had found her way back, she was allowed to stay, and her parents cared for her always."

The tingling intensified again. That seemed like a good sign.

"Show me the way to the city," Kaya said.

A small ball of light appeared. It hovered in front of her before moving forward. She followed it, trusting that the light would guide her through the forest.

Then it shot straight up.

The listeners were toying with her. They were punishing her after all.

Ignoring the light, she continued walking.

The light came down, circled around her a few times, and went back up into the air, where it hovered above her head.

"What do you want me to do?" Kaya demanded. "Climb a tree to get to Prima?"

The light bobbed up and down. The movement was reminiscent of a nod.

It was nonsense. She couldn't reach Prima by climbing a tree.

But she was pretty sure the listeners had promised not to punish her. If she truly believed they were good—and she did, deep down in her heart—she should trust them. She began climbing a tree.

It wasn't easy. Rain had made the trunk slick, and even with her boots back on, she got little traction. The light showed her where to place her hands, though, and the farther she went, the more branches there were for her to grab.

Even from this high up, she wouldn't have expected much of a view. What was there to see in a forest besides more trees? But the forest ended a short distance ahead. Beyond it lay a sprawling city, waves of streets and buildings leading to a giant fortress with towers that soared into the clouds.

Only one city could be that big. She'd reached Prima.

Chapter Nineteen

Kaya's plan had been simple: travel to Prima and free Hob. As she climbed down the tree, however, she realized that this had never been much of a plan at all. Free Hob *how*?

Before she attempted to storm the guildhall, she needed to figure out a strategy that had a chance of success. A little rest and a hot meal wouldn't hurt, either.

If she'd known where her aunt and uncle lived, she would have gone there first, but all she had was the name of her aunt, Fiola Li'Vow. She could not remember her uncle's name, and she had no idea where they lived or whether they would be inclined to help a niece they had never met. Perhaps Kaya could ask around about her aunt, but first she needed to take care of some more pressing needs—like finding food and shelter.

Back home, she would have sold a blanket or two to earn some money. She would have tried, anyway. She still had some of her blankets, but they were filthy and torn. No one would buy them.

"What can I sell?" she wondered aloud, casually addressing the listeners while she scanned the forest for ideas.

Her skin still tingled. Her last spell had gone well. She could tell another one, if she could think of one that was good enough.

A bird chirped behind her. She turned toward the sound—maybe she could down the bird with a rock and sell its meat—and was surprised to see a bush covered in rustberries.

It should have been too late in the year for rustberries, but these were perfectly ripe orangish-red specimens bursting with sweet juice. Kaya ate several handfuls. The rest she gathered in one of her dirty blankets, the closest thing she had to a container.

With her bounty in tow, she entered the city.

From her treetop view, Prima had looked enormous and beautiful, filled with colorful houses and towers that touched the clouds. Inside the city, the experience turned cramped and dirty. People shoved their way through the streets, which were too narrow. The smoke made Kaya cough. The noise made her head ache.

How could a place so large also be so crowded?

Kaya wandered the city, passing the well-kept shops, where women in beautiful dresses bought things like spices and lace, without stopping. No street vendors sold their goods, and Kaya imagined the shopkeepers paid good coin to keep it that way. She also avoided the sprawling houses decorated with marble statues and brightly colored windows. Those had to be where the wealthiest among the upper class lived, and a girl like Kaya would not be welcome.

The houses became less and less fancy as she walked. Soon, she came across some streets where no wealthy person would venture, where the scents of spirits mixed with the odors of human waste and where the people carried weapons they didn't bother to conceal. She hurried past this area, too, turning a corner and heading toward the sounds of drums and laughter.

Street performers were entertaining onlookers. Although the crowds they drew were larger, Kaya didn't think they were any more talented than the performers back in Verdan.

She kept walking until she found a good spot to hawk her berries, an area that was respectable enough to discourage robbery, but not so respectable that a mud-covered girl would get kicked out. The buildings looked modest and slightly rundown. The people looked modest and slightly rundown too. There were a few other vendors selling various items on the edge of the streets—walking canes, patches to mend clothes, and the like—bothered only by the occasional passing carriage that sprayed mud on them and their goods.

No one was selling fresh fruit. In fact, no one was selling food at all, not nearby. It struck Kaya as odd, since food was normally the one item that always had buyers. Hopefully, the lack of competition meant no one would mind her presence.

"Rustberries! Rustberries for sale!"

A man stopped. "Do you mean rustberry jam?"

Kaya showed him her blanket filled with berries. "They're fresh."

"Where did you get fresh rustberries so late in the year?"

"Trade secret." If she admitted to finding them in the forest just beyond the city borders, people might decide to find their own instead of buying from her. "Do you want them or not?"

He clearly did. He was practically salivating. "How much?"

"Three coins for a handful."

"They're normally two coins," the man said.

"They're normally not available this time of year. Take it or leave it."

The man bought the berries. Kaya was happy for the money, but she wondered whether she could get something else too: information. Not about Hob or the guild, of course. She couldn't go around asking strangers about that. The man might be able to help with something else, though.

"Do you know Fiola Li'Vow?" she asked. "I'm looking for her."

"Why?" Rustberry juice dripped down the man's chin as he spoke. "Who is she?"

"She's my—" Kaya stopped. On the off chance that the guild was looking for her, the girl who dared practice magic, she should avoid identifying herself. "I just need to talk to her. Do you know her?"

"Sorry. You should try selling the rest of your berries to the guild. They'd be perfect for Keen Im'Trif's wedding."

Kaya thanked him for his tip, but the last thing she wanted to do was introduce herself to the guild's grand magician.

More people bought rustberries. Some of them had baskets or bags that they used, but others made do with their hands. Kaya asked everyone about Fiola, but no one seemed to know her. In a city this big, that wasn't surprising.

Maybe it was for the best. Kaya had never even met her aunt. Asking her for help now would be quite presumptuous. Until she found Hob, she was on her own . . .

Only a few handfuls of rustberries remained. Kaya didn't bother yelling about them. Another customer—a woman holding an infant—was already approaching, and she looked quite eager. Word of the berries must have gotten around.

But when the woman spoke, it wasn't of fruit. "You're the spitting image of Fonna! You're her daughter, aren't you? You have to be! Kaya, right?"

Fonna was the name of Kaya's ma. "Who are you?" Kaya asked, though she suspected she knew.

"Fiola, your aunt. And this is Miker, your cousin." She nodded toward the infant she was carrying. "A friend told me someone was looking for me, but I didn't guess it would be you. What brings you to Prima? Where's Fonna?" A smile creased her face as her eyes searched the nearby street.

The smile wouldn't last, though, because her sister had died years ago.

Chapter Twenty

Kaya knew she had to tell Fiola, but she didn't want to break the news in the middle of the crowded street. "Can we go somewhere else? I've sold enough for the day."

"Do you really have fresh rustberries?" Fiola leaned over and whispered, "Sounds like a bit of magic to me. You've got your ma's talent, haven't you?"

"I, uh . . . Can we get out of here? I'm really tired." Not to mention suddenly terrified that others would make the same assumption. She hadn't used magic, not this time, but that wouldn't matter if the guild believed otherwise.

"Of course." The baby gurgled, and Fiola rocked back and forth to soothe him. "Just get your ma, and we'll go."

Kaya hesitated. "She's not here."

"Oh." Fiola frowned. "Your pa, then? Where is Chaul?"

"He's not here, either. I'm on my own. Well, Hob is around here somewhere. I came here to, uh, meet up with him."

"I don't understand. You're too young to be traveling on your own. She wouldn't—" Fiola stopped. She must have seen the sadness on Kaya's face. "Your ma never wrote very often, but she did write. She told me about you and your brother Hob, how you were doing, how proud she was when Hob got accepted for a guild apprenticeship. It was soon after that, about five years ago, that the letters stopped. I tried to tell myself she was just busy or that Chaul had made her stop, but it wasn't that, was it?"

Kaya shook her head. "They got sick, Ma and Pa both."

"And you and Hob have been on your own ever since. I'm so sorry." She wiped the tears that had started streaming down her cheeks. "Why didn't you come here to live with me? I would have been happy to take you in."

"Hob had just started the apprenticeship. He got a stipend." Truth be told, they'd never discussed the possibility of moving to Prima. Hob had said he'd take care of them, and that was that.

"He *got* a stipend?" Fiola echoed, emphasizing the past tense. "Doesn't he still get it? Did something happen?"

Kaya opened her mouth to answer, but faced with the dilemma of lying to her aunt or confessing to a relative she hardly knew, she didn't know what to say.

Fiola wiped her tear-moistened eyes with her sleeve. "You're right. We should get out of here. Do you have a place to stay?"

"No."

"You do now. Let's get going." Fiola smiled through her tears. Miker awoke and, perhaps sensing the gloomy mood, sobbed loudly.

—

Fiola rented an apartment, of course. The lower class wasn't allowed to own property, meaning they always had to rent or—

like the family in the woods—squat. But Fiola's apartment was much larger than the space Kaya and Hob had shared.

There were listeners there too. The second Kaya stepped inside, her skin tingled.

"What does your husband do?" Kaya asked, hoping it wasn't too prying. Fiola's husband was her uncle, after all.

"He died, right before Miker was born." Fiola's eyes were moist as she said this, but that might have been because she was still teary over the news of her sister.

"You're on your own? How do you—" She looked around at the spacious apartment. She also noticed Fiola's dress, which was simple but free of holes and frayed edges. She had ribbons braided into her long hair, the type Anny sold in Verdan. "How do you manage?"

"It's time for Miker's nap. Come with me to put him down, and I'll show you." Fiola led Kaya into the other room. There was a bed, where Fiola must have slept, and a small crib for Miker.

Fiola passed the bed and the crib on her way to a shelf. On it were several potted plants. "I sell these."

They were herbs, all different types. Kaya inhaled the savory aromas. "How do you get them to grow in here? There's no light."

"How do you think?" Fiola put Miker down in the crib. She had to stretch her arms to do so, allowing a piece of blue string to peek out from under her sleeve.

"You're a member of MAGE!" Kaya clasped her hands over her mouth. She shouldn't yell such things.

Fiola nodded, unashamed and unafraid. "Something only a member of MAGE would know."

"Me? No. I'm not a member. Hob—" She stopped.

"Ah, yes, of course Hob is a member. I'd expect nothing less from Fonna's son. Where is he, anyway? Did he get suspended from the guild?"

"No. Not exactly. He's—" She hesitated again. Could she trust this woman? Her aunt. A MAGE member. If not her, then who? And time was running out for Hob. Kaya couldn't refuse help just because she was afraid. "The guild imprisoned him. But he didn't do anything wrong. They imprisoned him for—for—" Her words caught in her throat.

"For being a MAGE member, I suspect, or else for teaching you magic." Fiola gave a dismissive wave of her hand. "Oh, don't look so surprised! Obviously, he's taught you a thing or two. How else could you have made it all the way here on your own? Or grown those rustberries this late in the year?"

"I didn't use magic to make those rustberries grow," Kaya insisted, not bothering to deny the rest of it. Her aunt might as well have been a mind reader, as perceptive as she was. "I just found them."

"After saying that you needed them? Or something like them?"

Kaya nodded, confused as to how her aunt had guessed—or why it mattered. She *had* wondered aloud what she could sell, but what did that have to do with anything?

"The listeners heard you," Fiola said, "and they helped you."

"But I didn't tell a story."

"If the listeners like you, sometimes they'll help you without a story if they know what you need. The guild likes to think of them as servants. I like to think of them as friends."

The scent of herbs became suddenly stronger. The plants were growing right before Kaya's eyes—as if to offer proof of Fiola's claims. "Hob never told me that."

"That's the fault of the guild training. No matter how much he's passed on to you, there's a lot you still have to learn about listeners and story magic."

Kaya had begun to suspect as much. But there was no time for this. "The guild is going to execute Hob on the thirtieth of Harkia. That's only seven days from now. I need to help him escape before then."

"Do you have a plan?"

"Only to sneak into the guildhall and let him out."

"Which guildhall?" Fiola asked. "The guild has several buildings throughout Prima, including two large guildhalls. Both have a cell or two for prisoners. Do you know where he's being kept?"

Kaya shook her head. Her plan was even more pathetic than she'd realized.

"I may be able to help," Fiola said. "I have friends in the guild. At the very least, they'll provide us with information. While we wait, you should get some food and some rest. You must be exhausted after your journey, and you'll be of no use to your brother in such a weary state. We'll get you cleaned up too."

"Thank you," Kaya said, and if her words sounded uncertain, it wasn't because she didn't mean them. As difficult as her journey had been, she knew the hardest part was still to come.

Chapter
Twenty-One

The next morning, Kaya lay on the mat that had been put in the main room for her. Her dress was hanging to dry after being washed and mended, and she was wearing one of her aunt's old nightgowns. It was too large for Kaya, but it was soft and warm, and the mat was comfortable. Nevertheless, she hadn't slept well.

Hob's execution would be held in six days.

It wasn't right. The guild had no legal authority to execute people—but who was going to stop them? The king? He never interfered in their affairs, which was probably wise. Kings who did never lasted long, not according to Hob, who had relayed the history with anger—and sometimes a hint of admiration—in his voice.

"Good morning," Fiola said, her cheerful tone interrupting Kaya's grave thoughts. Fiola was holding Miker, who looked just as chipper as his ma. "Here's the plan for the day. First, I'm going to fix us some gruel for breakfast. Then I want to ask a friend to look into your brother's situation. While we wait for him to get back to us, we'll spend the day practicing magic."

The entire day? "Aren't you worried about bad luck?" Kaya asked.

"Why? Because I'm a woman?" Fiola put Miker down on the floor so she could roll up the mat. "The guild just says that so they'll have an excuse for not accepting women. Hob must have told you that before he started teaching you."

"Yes, but . . ." Kaya thought back to everything that had gone wrong since her first story. "A lot of bad things happened after I started telling stories."

"Sometimes bad things happen. It doesn't mean you caused them. I do story magic all the time, and I haven't suffered any misfortune because of it."

"Your husband died." The words slipped out before Kaya could stop them. She wished she could shove the sentence back down her throat, but it was too late. She'd accused Fiola of causing her husband's death. She wouldn't be surprised if Fiola never spoke to her again.

But Fiola didn't seem angry—only sad. "That was horrible, yes, but it wasn't because of the stories. And neither is what's happened to Hob."

Kaya thought it was nice of Fiola to say so, but also that she couldn't really know. Even if it wasn't bad luck for a girl to do story magic, it was still banned. The guild had found out, and they'd taken Hob because of it. They were going to kill him, and it was her fault, with or without bad luck.

"We'll go to the lake to practice," Fiola insisted. "You'll need to have the listeners on your side if you're going to cross the guild. At least we know they won't be on the guild's side."

"What do you mean?" Kaya asked. "Of course the listeners will be on the guild's side."

Fiola frowned. "Didn't Hob tell you? The listeners are angry with the guild. They've stopped doing magic for them. Most listeners have, anyway, for most guild members. A few listeners continue to help their favorites."

So the rumor Anny had heard was true. "Hob mentioned that the guild had secrets, secrets that could lead to their undoing, but he didn't say what they were."

"He was probably trying to keep you safe," Fiola said, though she was still frowning. "Can you mind Miker while I get our food ready?"

Kaya agreed, but Miker didn't need much minding. He had a set of wooden blocks and was very content to play with them. Kaya just watched.

And listened. Fiola was telling a story.

"There once lived a squirrel," she said without bothering to greet the listeners, although the strong tingling Kaya felt meant they were near. "It was a strange-looking squirrel, with a hard, sharp nose and curious blue fur. Its front legs weren't right, either, and everyone suspected this was why its own ma had abandoned it.

"Another squirrel, who had her own kits to care for, took pity on the sad creature and decided to raise it. The strange blue squirrel tried to keep up with its adoptive brothers and sisters, who scampered up and down the trees, but its deformed limbs meant it was no good at climbing. The crueler among its adopted siblings made fun of the poor thing, but it refused to give up.

"One day, it managed to climb a tree all the way up to a tall limb. Unfortunately, climbing down was even more difficult than climbing up. It fell, and as it fell, it was sure it was going to die, but at the last moment, its front limbs stretched out. Its malformed legs started flapping, and it rose into the air. Flying away, it realized it wasn't a deformed squirrel at all. It was a bird."

After finishing the story, Fiola was quiet.

"That was cute," Kaya said. "But why did you tell a story with no magical words? What's the point if there's no spell?"

Fiola shrugged. "I enjoy telling stories, and the listeners enjoy listening. I don't have to get something out of it every time. Like I said, the listeners are my friends, not my servants. Besides, isn't that tingling thanks enough?"

Indeed, the tingling had intensified. It felt good on Kaya's scalp, almost like a massage. The purposeless story still struck her as strange, though. She had never heard of anyone who wasn't doing magic telling a story. In fact, the guild forbade it—and for good reason.

"Isn't it dangerous?" Kaya asked. On her long and lonely journey, she'd fallen into the habit of talking to the listeners, but stories were a different matter entirely.

"Why would it be dangerous?"

"It confuses the listeners."

Fiola laughed. "Why would a story confuse them? Do you think the listeners are daft?"

"No, but they can get angry if they don't like the story," said Kaya, more than a little irritated. She didn't appreciate being laughed at. It reminded her of the way Hob sometimes made fun of her questions—only with Hob, she didn't mind. Usually. Or she *did* mind, but he could get away with it because he was so smart and he took care of her. "You just said the listeners are mad at the guild. They could get mad at us, too, if we tell the wrong stories. We take the risk when we need something, but only then."

Fiola dismissed this with a wave of her hand. "The listeners can get angry, yes, but it takes more than a weak story. And they don't punish people for bad tales. That's just nonsense the guild spreads. Think about it. Have you ever seen a listener strike down a storyteller?"

"Well, no," Kaya admitted. Listeners had ignored her at times, but they'd never actively hurt her. "Not personally. But I've heard about it. Someone told the same story twice, and a listener struck the magician dead. Another magician was blinded for his dull tale. And then there's the apprentice who had his tongue ripped out. Nothing really bad has ever happened to me, not that I could be sure the listeners had caused, but I think it could. The listeners have ignored some of my stories. They must be getting bored."

Fiola, who had stopped laughing, covered the pot she'd been stirring and took a seat on the floor between Kaya and Miker. Her expression had turned serious, and Kaya was sure this meant her fears were justified. The listeners no longer cared for her stories. If she didn't regain their favor soon, she'd feel their wrath.

"When did they ignore you?" Fiola asked. "Tell me exactly what happened."

Kaya had no trouble recalling the first incident. "I was walking through the forest, and I was hungry. I'd eaten fruit and mushrooms, but I wanted something heartier, so I asked the listener to catch and cook some fish for me. The listener didn't do it."

"The listeners won't kill," Fiola said. "Not fish. Not people. Not anything with a heartbeat. That's all. They weren't unhappy with your storytelling skills. They didn't punish you. They just won't do certain things."

"Hob never told me they wouldn't even kill fish."

"The guild might not have told him yet, especially if he's still an apprentice. People aren't as afraid of the guild once they realize story magic has such limits. The listeners are kind creatures. As long as you don't ask them to do anything harmful—or do anything to harm them—they'll always be there for you."

"That's not true." Kaya told her aunt what had happened in the strange town she'd encountered, the one where Belma and Villy had called her bedeviled and put her in the pillory. "I needed to do a spell so I could escape, but the listeners wouldn't come, not even when I lit some incense before it was taken from me. Normally, they're almost always around, but when I really needed them, they stayed away."

"I've heard of that town. It's called Silenton, and it's surrounded by barrier metal. Listeners can't enter. Or maybe they could, if they wanted, since the metal doesn't completely cover the town, but they don't. Listeners hate barrier metal. It frightens them, and they don't go near it—not on purpose anyway."

"Barrier metal?" Kaya had never heard the term before. "Is that what that strange line around the town was? I thought it was left over from an old wall or something. How does it work?"

Fiola sighed. "It's a horrible thing. Let's not talk about it right now. Are you hungry? The gruel should be ready. I'm sorry I can't provide anything fancier, but it's hard to find food these days, even if you have money for it. The guild depended on the listeners to help crops grow, and now that the listeners won't cooperate with the guild, the crops are suffering. Everyone's suffering."

"I don't need anything fancy." Kaya could smell the gruel, and if she hadn't been hungry already, the delicious scent would have changed her mind.

Fiola handed her a bowl of gruel. "I added a bit of herbs, courtesy of the listeners. Hope you like it."

Kaya loved it. "Thank you, Fiola." And because she knew they were listening, she added, "Thank you, listeners."

But she couldn't help feeling disappointed. The listeners had limits. What if those limits meant they couldn't help her save her brother?

Chapter Twenty-Two

Beneath a heavy layer of gray clouds, Prima was bustling. People walked quickly, passing each other without greeting, while large men stood guard at the street corners. Some of the men wore the guild's uniform. Others wore black and gold, the king's colors.

"Are there always so many guards?" Kaya whispered.

"No," Fiola said. "At least, there didn't used to be. Security's gotten tighter as food has gotten scarcer. People are starting to catch on to the guild's problems with the listeners too. It won't be too long before the mumblings turn into rebellions. Stay here for a moment."

After handing Miker to Kaya, Fiola walked over to one of the men wearing a guild uniform.

Sweaty panic gripped Kaya. Fiola was turning her into the guild. She had to run—but she was still holding Miker.

Kaya forced herself to take a deep breath. Why would Fiola hand over her baby to a person she intended to betray? She wasn't turning Kaya in. She was asking a friend to look into Hob's situation, exactly as she'd promised.

So why couldn't Kaya listen? Unless there was something Fiola didn't want Kaya to hear.

Kaya was too far to eavesdrop but close enough to watch their faces. Their expressions ranged from happy to polite, with only occasional flickers of seriousness. This probably meant little, except that they knew they were being watched—by Kaya or by others.

When Fiola returned, she whispered, "He doesn't know much about your brother, but he'll ask around and get back to us. I told him that we don't have much time."

Kaya nodded. What else could she do? The guild had taken Hob prisoner because he had taught her magic. Now he suffered while she got to waste time at the lake.

She didn't know why Fiola had decided they should practice magic at the lake, of all places. It would be safer to practice in the privacy of Fiola's apartment. The best Kaya could figure was that it was an excuse to get her to relax. She couldn't do that, though, not while Hob awaited his execution.

—

The lake wasn't as crowded as Kaya had expected—unlike the rest of Prima—probably because of the weather. As soon as they got there, a light rain drizzled down upon them. Then the gentle trickle became a heavy downpour, and the few men who had been fishing packed up their equipment and left. "We should do the same," Kaya said, gesturing to them.

"Nonsense." Fiola put her son on the muddy ground. "We just got here."

"Won't Miker get sick?"

"From the fresh air and rain? He's more likely to catch something in the crowded, filthy streets than he is here. Besides, he's bundled up all nice and toasty." She paused. "Are you okay?"

"Yes." Kaya tried not to shiver. It wasn't even winter yet, and the trek to Prima should have toughened her up some, but she was as sensitive to the chill as ever. Her bony body simply didn't have enough fat to keep her warm. It didn't help that Prima's climate was slightly colder than Verdan's. Soon, it might even start to snow. "I'm fine."

"Good, because there's something you need to see. Come over here." She walked to the water's edge. "Do you want to tell the story, or should I?"

Kaya stood next to Fiola. The lake water seeped into her boots. Because the rainwater was already doing the same, it didn't do much harm, but it didn't do any good, either. "What story? Do you need a spell?"

"Not exactly, although we can do it that way. Like I said, I want to show you something."

Kaya was getting tired of these cryptic statements. Fiola wanted to show her something. Okay. But *what*? And why here? Kaya didn't want to be rude, though, not when her aunt was being so generous. "You can tell the story."

Fiola stretched her arms out, as if the rain felt good on her skin. More likely, she was reveling in the tingling sensation, which was as strong here as it tended to be in her home. "Gather 'round, listeners," she said, instead of the normal welcome Hob and the other guild members always used. "Once, there was a boy who was very lonely. The other children his age thought he was strange because he laughed at the wrong things and spoke at the wrong times, and they shunned him for it.

"Truth be told, the boy didn't care much for them, either. Nevertheless, he was lonely. He wanted friends. He tried being nice to other children, even when they were mean to him. They threw things at him, and he offered to share his food with them. They called him names, and he complimented their clothes. Unfortunately, this didn't work. If anything, it convinced the children that he was even stranger than they'd realized.

"Unable to find friends in the city, the boy took to wandering the woods. One day, he found a blood wolf pup that had gotten stuck under a fallen tree. The boy was afraid of blood wolves, but this was only a pup, and he felt sorry for it. He lifted the tree, and the pup ran off.

"Knowing that there were blood wolves around, the boy no longer felt safe in the woods, but he couldn't stand to stay in the city, where the other children tormented him, so he returned to the woods the next day. His fears were soon justified. An entire pack of blood wolves surrounded him.

"He ran, but he tripped over a branch and stumbled. The blood wolves drew closer. The boy tried to stand, but his leg was hurt. He closed his eyes and cried, sure that the wolves would devour him. But he didn't feel the wolves' teeth tearing at his skin. He felt their soft faces nuzzling him.

"The boy opened his eyes. The wolves couldn't speak with words, but they could communicate with their eyes and their bodies. 'We are your friends,' they were saying, and the boy was never alone again."

Fiola paused for a moment. Then she repeated the words, "We are your friends."

Kaya took a step back. *We are your friends.* The story made them words of power, but what were they supposed to do? Make Kaya think Fiola and Miker were friends? That sounded like mind control.

Hob had said such magic lay beyond the powers of the listeners, but what if he'd been wrong about that too?

If Fiola could manipulate Kaya's thoughts, then Kaya could influence the thoughts of the guild members.

But Kaya didn't feel mind controlled. Her opinion of Fiola hadn't changed. Her aunt was good at magic and very knowledgeable. She was nice and interesting, but not quite as serious or direct as Kaya would have liked.

More than anything else, Kaya saw her aunt as a stranger. And Miker was an adorable baby.

If the spell had been meant to make Kaya see these two as friends, it had failed.

"Come see," Fiola said. She was looking at the lake. Something splashed in the water. Kaya approached to see what it was, expecting to find a fish or a turtle.

It was no fish. It was no turtle. It hardly seemed to be anything at all.

The water sparkled beautifully. Kaya reached out a hand. She wanted to touch the glittering water, but she was afraid she would ruin the effect. Her fingers hovered just above the surface of the lake.

The water reached up to touch her hand. A warm, tingling sensation spread from her hand up her arm.

"They like you," Fiola said.

"They? Who are they?"

"The listeners, of course. They're water-bound."

"Wat—" Kaya began, but before she could finish, Miker's scream interrupted her.

Miker was in the water. He was drowning.

Chapter Twenty-Three

Kaya ran into the lake after Miker. He couldn't have been in the water very long—but how many seconds did it take to drown? If the water got much deeper, she might find out firsthand.

She reached out to grab Miker, but her hands clasped at nothing. Miker had jumped up out of the way.

Which was impossible. People couldn't jump on water any more than they could walk on it. But there Miker was, bouncing on the surface of the lake. His screams were that of an ecstatic child, not a frightened one.

The water around his feet shimmered brilliantly.

"The listeners like him too," Fiola said, wading into the lake behind Kaya.

"Aren't you worried? He could drown—"

She shook her head, smiling. "The listeners wouldn't let that happen."

Perhaps, but . . . "He could freeze," Kaya said. The boy's layers wouldn't keep him warm when he was soaking wet.

"Are you cold?" Fiola asked.

Kaya had to admit that she was not. "Why is the water so warm?"

"The listeners, of course. They can take a physical form by binding to water. They don't do it all the time, but they know I like to watch them sparkle. So does Miker, the little terror." She splashed a handful of water at her son, who giggled in response. "That's why he crawled into the lake, I'm sure."

Kaya couldn't believe it. "Does the guild know? Hob never mentioned—"

"Oh, the guild knows." Fiola's expression turned grave, almost angry. "They devised a plan not so long ago. They fed dogs food laced with powdered barrier metal. The metal accumulated in their bodies, and when the guild thought there was enough, they filled water with conjuring herb to encourage listeners to become water-bound. Then they made the dogs drink the water—and the listeners with it."

"The hounds! I saw them. But they were evil. They tried to hurt me. How could they be listeners? You said listeners would never hurt anyone."

"They wouldn't, not normally. Listeners can't abide being trapped. The barrier metal kept them inside the dogs, and it was torture for them. Over time, it twisted and corrupted them. Those things used to be listeners, but they've become something else. Something that should never have been."

"Why did the guild do it?" Kaya had little love for the guild these days, but she couldn't imagine they would be cruel for no reason.

"They thought they'd be able to control the dogs. It was supposed to be a way to do magic more easily, without the trouble of storytelling."

"But telling stories isn't that hard," Kaya said. "It's not always easy for me, but Hob doesn't have any trouble. No guild members do."

"True—for simple commands at least. More complicated commands require more complicated stories, and sometimes the listeners don't understand what's being asked of them. There are things the listeners won't do, too, and the guild thought they might force them this way." Fiola shook her head in dismay. "But the listeners were too terrified and too angry to do anything. And once the other listeners discovered what was happening, most of them refused to do magic for the guild. Only a few guild members have managed to stay on good terms with the listeners."

"So they trapped the listeners, just to make magic a little easier. That . . . That's awful." Kaya looked at the listeners glistening in the water around her, and it made her sick. How could anyone turn something so beautiful into something so awful? It was unforgiveable. "Why don't people know? The hounds live in the forest right next to Verdan."

"The guild won't admit their mistakes, and they won't give away their secrets, either, especially now that they're weak. They silence anyone who finds out. Not that it's usually necessary. Most people who encounter the dogs are killed by them. How did you escape?"

"I told a story." Kaya's heart raced as she recalled the terrifying moment—her stuck in the tree while the hounds howled below and the wind nearly pried her from the branches. "I assumed a listener heard me, but could it have been the hounds themselves?"

Fiola considered this. "Possibly. I honestly don't know if anyone else has tried telling stories to the poor creatures . . . We should head back. You'll want to get dry, and I need to prepare some herbs for the market."

As they walked back to Fiola's house, Kaya contemplated what she had learned. If Hob knew about the hounds—and he must have, having worked so close to the fields where the hounds prowled—he would have been outraged. It could have been one of the reasons he'd decided to join MAGE.

The guild wouldn't get away with what they'd done. Kaya wouldn't let them.

Chapter Twenty-Four

*F*iola had some extra yarn lying around her apartment, as well as a pair of knitting needles, so Kaya decided to knit a blanket to sell at the market. Some more money would be nice, although she didn't actually expect the blanket to sell. She just wanted something to occupy her mind while she waited for news about Hob.

Only a few hours had passed since Fiola had asked her magician friend for information, but Kaya couldn't help staring at the door anytime she heard a noise outside. Was it the man? Did he know how to save Hob?

Every once in a while, Fiola took a break from her own work with her herbs to check in on Kaya.

"That's beautiful," Fiola said, pointing to the blanket—even though Kaya had barely started it.

"That's because the yarn's so nice." It was a deep green, evenly dyed and plush, and it must have been expensive.

"Your technique's good. Better than mine." Fiola pointed to the booties currently keeping Miker's feet warm. "Have you tried making things other than blankets? Scarves, booties, and mittens would all use less yarn, and I think they'd be more popular."

She was right, Kaya realized. Blankets took a lot of yarn. If she made smaller items and sold them for the same price, she would make more money—assuming anything sold. "I suppose I could turn this into a scarf. I haven't done booties or mittens before, but I could try."

The scarves were easy. Kaya was a fast knitter, and she finished two in less time than a single blanket would have taken. The booties took more work. Even after getting some tips from Fiola, and even though she was using Miker's booties as a guide, she still had to undo her work and start over several times before getting them right. It was late when she finished two pairs that satisfied her, and she decided to tackle mittens another day.

"You've got real talent," Fiola said, examining the booties. "We should get you some more yarn tomorrow. Have you ever tried anything else, like weaving or embroidery? You could get a spinner to make your own yarn, and I think you'd be good with a loom."

A loom. Kaya had always wanted one, but . . . "I can't afford a loom."

Fiola dismissed this with a wave of her hand. "I'd be happy to buy one for you. It would be a good investment. You could do quite well here."

"That's kind of you," Kaya said, "but I won't be here very long."

"Where will you go?"

Kaya had no idea. After she helped Hob escape, they couldn't stay in Prima. They couldn't return home, either, where the guild would look for them. They'd have to go somewhere else, maybe sneak aboard a boat and sail as far away as possible. Kaya had thought about this on many a sleepless night, but she hadn't made any plans. By then, Hob would be back in charge. "I'm not sure."

"Well, you're welcome to stay here. I know I must seem like a stranger to you, but you remind me so much of your ma." She took Kaya's hand. "We are family."

"Why did you and Ma stop talking?"

"Your pa didn't like me. No, that's not fair. He liked me fine. He just worried about your ma. He thought I was dangerous. He didn't want any trouble with the guild. That's why he moved the family away from Prima. He wanted to move to Silenton, but Fonna wouldn't have it." She wiped away a tear and smiled.

"Why did he think you were dangerous?" Kaya asked. "Is it because you did story magic?"

"Yes. And no. I was mischievous as a child, and I didn't care for the guild. I played tricks on the magicians, using magic to move their stuff around or to spill things on their clothes. I had fun torturing them." She laughed. "Tell me about your brother, will you?"

Kaya's face brightened. "He's smart and kind too. He . . . He . . ." Kaya tried to think of an example, something he'd done that showed just how wonderful he was. But in all her recent memories, he was yelling at someone, or criticizing her, or putting his muddy feet on the table she'd just cleaned. "He got accepted into the guild when he was only twelve."

"Yes. And he took care of both of you. That was very brave of such a young boy. Your ma and pa would be proud."

Kaya nodded, barely paying attention. She was still trying to recall a pleasant memory of her brother. She'd always thought of him as smart and kind. His story magic skills proved some intelligence, but what of his kindness?

He used to be nicer. When Kaya was little, Hob had taught her how to run and swim and climb and hide. He said he just wanted a decent hide-and-seek partner, and they used to play all the time, but Kaya suspected that he was also looking out for her. He wanted her to be able to get out of trouble if she was ever in danger. He took care of her, even back then.

Then their parents died, and he no longer had time for games. He became serious and angry, but he still took care of Kaya.

She supposed it had been nice of him to teach her magic, even if he had been insulting about it most of the time—constantly pointing out how easy it was, that even a half-wit could do it. He always had some sort of criticism for her.

Fiola checked on dinner and announced that it was done.

Herbs seasoned the stew to perfection. Kaya ate seconds, followed by thirds. It was so good that not even Hob could have found anything to complain about.

Or perhaps he *would* have found something. He might have said the stew was too hot or else not hot enough. Chairs were never comfortable enough for him, and nights were never quiet enough.

No matter how hard she tried to impress him, Kaya never succeeded.

But he'd be impressed when she rescued him. That was all that mattered.

—

Kaya couldn't sleep that night. Any time spent sleeping was time wasted, and her brother had so little time left.

She got up. Careful not to make any noise, she rifled through the cooking supplies, then the baubles that decorated a shelf.

She wasn't sure what she was looking for. Fiola had shown her nothing but kindness, but Kaya couldn't shake the feeling that she was hiding something. Besides, kindness didn't mean goodness. Belma had been kind in the beginning.

A wooden chest sat in one corner of the apartment, covered by a piece of lace and topped with cooking pans. At first, Kaya had mistaken it for a table. She opened it. It contained clothes, but not Fiola's. These were men's clothes, green and decorated with the emblem of a leaf. They were a guild magician's uniform.

Blood stained the collar.

Kaya put the uniform back and returned the lace and cooking pans. She went to her mat and closed her eyes, but her mind raced.

Chapter Twenty-Five

Kaya had been tempted to run away before Fiola woke. But where would she have gone? And Fiola had promised to help rescue Hob. Kaya couldn't risk losing that help, not unless she was absolutely sure.

Not that there was much room for doubt. Fiola kept a bloody guild uniform hidden in a chest. She was clearly a murderer.

But perhaps there were special circumstances. The guild magician had attacked her, for example, and she'd had to defend herself. Something like that.

Or not. Fiola had admitted to playing tricks on magicians— "torturing them," she'd said. She didn't like the guild. What if one of her tricks had gone wrong?

Kaya would have to ask her. There was no other way to learn the truth.

A private apartment was no place to confront a murderer, though. Kaya ate breakfast as if nothing were wrong. When Fiola said it was time to go to the market, Kaya smiled pleasantly.

Kaya carried Miker, while Fiola carried the herbs and knitted goods.

"What a dear you are," Fiola said, oblivious to the tension Kaya felt.

Kaya waited until they were on a busy street. If the conversation went badly, she would be able to put down Miker and disappear into the crowd.

In a low voice, she asked, "Why do you have a guild magician's uniform in your chest? Did you kill the owner? Is that what MAGE members do?"

Fiola stopped walking. Her head tilted slightly to one side. "Kill? Why, no, what would make you think that? The uniform belonged to my husband, of course."

Kaya stopped walking too. "Your husband was a guild member? You said you didn't like the guild."

"That was when I was a child. My husband was a guild member and MAGE member, just like Hob."

"But there was blood on the collar."

Fiola pressed her lips into a flat line. It looked like she was trying to hold back tears. "He had a horrible cough. I should have cleaned the blood, but I couldn't bear to look at it. I suppose it's too late to get the stain out now."

Miker busied himself playing with Kaya's hair, happily ignorant of the sadness around him.

"I . . . I . . ." Kaya wasn't sure what to say. She'd just accused her aunt of murder, and now the truth seemed so obvious. Of course the clothes had belonged to her husband. But there was still one thing Kaya didn't understand. "If he was a magician, why didn't he just tell a story to heal himself? Why didn't *you* tell a story?"

"We tried. I think the listeners tried too. They like healing people, but some illnesses are beyond their control."

"When our parents died, Hob blamed the guild," Kaya said. "I'm sorry I looked through your things."

"It's fine," Fiola said. "You don't really know me yet, but I hope we can change that. In the meantime, your brother is a member of MAGE, remember. You can trust us. We don't go around killing people, I promise."

Kaya nodded. "I'd like to meet them. Maybe they know something about Hob."

"If they do, my friend will find out for us. We just have to be patient."

"Hob only has five days!" Kaya shouted. In a hushed voice, she added, "I need to do something. I could go to the guildhall, both of them, and any other buildings I need to, and see where they have him—"

"And what?" Fiola asked. "Break him out? Without a plan? Without any help from MAGE? You'll get caught, and how will that help your brother?"

"I have to do something."

Fiola held up the booties Kaya had knitted. "You can sell these. You and your brother will need the coins, right?"

Kaya nodded. Starting a new life would be hard, and without Hob's stipend from the guild, they'd need a new source of income.

They had come to a nice spot in the market, well trafficked but reasonably clean. Kaya stopped. "This looks good," she said to Fiola before yelling, "Scarves! Herbs! Booties for your baby's feet!"

Fiola smiled, but it wasn't her normal cheery expression. It was more of a cringe. "Oh, no, we don't need to do that here. We can sell at the shop."

Kaya's mouth fell open. "You have your own shop?"

"My friend Amila S'Ford owns it, but she lets me use a corner. I'm sure she won't mind you selling, too, but we'll have to ask first."

Fiola was friends with a lady in the upper class. That was almost as good as belonging to it herself. No wonder her apartment was so nice.

—

The shop was large and nicely decorated, with curtains on the windows and rugs on the floor. "Hello, Amila. This is my niece, Kaya. Kaya, this is Amila S'Ford. Amila, do you mind if Kaya joins me today? She's made some lovely scarves and booties and would like to sell them."

"Oh, yes, of course." Amila took the booties Kaya was holding. "These are quite nice. Rosini! Aren't you looking for some booties?" This last part was directed at a woman on the other side of the shop.

Rosini confirmed that she was still in need of some booties for her twins, and several minutes later, Kaya had sold half of her merchandise. Halfway through the day, she'd sold the rest.

"We'll get you more yarn," Fiola promised. "And perhaps that loom too."

"Thanks," Kaya said, not mentioning again that she wouldn't be around long enough to use it. It was already the twenty-fifth of Harkia. She only had five more days to find Hob. Then, as much as she would have liked to stay with her aunt, in a warm apartment with all the yarn she could want, she'd have to flee with her brother.

Fiola knew that. So why did she offer the loom? Was she trying to tempt Kaya to abandon her brother, or did she assume Kaya would fail in her rescue attempts? If she never learned where Hob was being held, she'd have no reason to leave.

But Kaya would learn Hob's location. If Fiola's friends didn't provide the information she needed soon, she would go out that night on her own. She'd done it before, when she'd entered the guildhall in Verdan. It would be harder in a city the size of Prima, where the guild had multiple buildings, but she wouldn't give up.

—

When Amila closed her shop that evening, Fiola and Kaya walked back to Fiola's apartment. Fiola was tired—she'd done a good deal more business than Kaya—so Kaya carried Miker again.

When the apartment came into view, she stopped mid-step. Fearful that she might drop Miker, she overcompensated by squeezing him tighter.

She wouldn't have to wait any longer for news about her brother. She wouldn't have to venture out on her own in search of information, either. The guild member Fiola had spoken to was waiting outside the apartment.

Chapter Twenty-Six

"Klar," Fiola said, addressing the guild member waiting outside her front door. "Have you been waiting long?"

"Not at all," he replied. On the left side of his face, an old scar ran from the middle of his forehead to his jaw. His skin was pale, and his hair was long. "I was just hoping to buy some herbs from you, if you have any left."

"Yes, but not on me. I sold everything I brought to the shop. Why don't you step inside, and I'll get you taken care of?" Fiola opened the door to her apartment.

Klar was a large man, and he had to stoop a little to enter. While Fiola, Kaya, and Miker followed him inside, Kaya's face grew hot with anger. *Herbs?* He'd stopped by for herbs? She'd nearly panicked at the sight of him, sure that he had news of Hob, but no one even bothered to mention her brother. Didn't they care? Maybe not the man, Klar, but Fiola at least should have shown some concern.

Kaya put Miker down on the floor near his toy blocks. "Isn't somebody going to talk about Hob? I only have five days to free him."

Fiola shushed her while shutting the door.

"That's why I'm here," Klar said.

"This isn't the type of conversation we can have outside," Fiola said. "Or inside, for that matter, if you're shouting. The herbs were just a cover." She turned to Klar. "Although you're welcome to some if you'd like."

"How about some of that herbal tea you make?" Klar sat down on a chair. He seemed comfortable in the apartment, as if he'd been there before. "Hob A'Dor is being held captive by the guild."

Kaya already knew that. "Is his execution still planned for the thirtieth of Harkia?"

"Yes. Normally, executions are carried out immediately, but Keen Im'Trif wanted to interrogate him. That's why the execution is being held after the grand magician's wedding." Klar hesitated. "Do you know what Hob did?"

Kaya's shoulders tensed. Klar was there to help, supposedly, but so far he hadn't been any help at all. How much did Fiola know about him? He was a guild magician, and the guild was trying to learn about Hob. What if Klar was gathering information for the guild?

"Go ahead and tell him what you know," Fiola said. She handed Klar a cup with one hand. Her other hand rested on his shoulder. "He's a member of MAGE, and he's never turned his back on other members. He'll keep your secrets like he's kept mine."

Kaya relaxed, if only slightly. She took a seat across from Klar. "Hob taught me magic. I performed a spell in the market in Verdan. The guild must have found out."

"Maybe so," Klar said, "but that's not why the guild has brought him here. The grand magician doesn't waste his time interrogating people for such common matters. What else could he have done?"

"He's a member of MAGE," Kaya said. "Maybe the grand magician wants information on the group."

Klar shook his head. "It's not that, either. I spoke to someone who has a brother in Verdan." Klar took a deep breath, like he was steeling himself, then looked Kaya in the eyes. "I'm sorry to be the bearer of bad news, but MAGE has refused to help Hob because, apparently, he's done something horrible. I'm trying to find out more, but I promise no MAGE member would ever abandon someone whose only crimes were being a member and teaching magic to his little sister. Whatever he's done, it's bad enough to put him on the wrong side of both MAGE and the guild."

"That can't be right," Kaya said. "Hob would never do anything horrible."

"My information is incomplete. It could also be incorrect." Klar didn't sound convinced by his own words.

"It is," Kaya insisted. "Grey—that's his friend—Grey said the guild went after Hob because of me. If I turned myself in and told them everything they want to know, do you think they'd let him go?"

"No." Klar's response was as fast as it was firm.

"But you said the grand magician is interrogating Hob. I could offer information in exchange for his freedom."

"The grand magician doesn't work that way. He doesn't care what children have to say, and he doesn't make deals with girls. At best, he'd ignore you. At worst, he'd execute you alongside your brother." He sipped from his cup. "And I told you: this isn't about you or MAGE. Whatever your brother did, it had to be something far less common to warrant Keen's attention."

"He didn't do anything horrible," Kaya insisted. Maybe he was rude sometimes—a lot of the time—but he was still a good person. "He cares about people. He's always talking about how he wants to use magic to help others. He would never do anything bad."

"What about freeing him through other means?" Fiola said. "I was thinking that MAGE might be able to put something together."

Klar shook his head. "MAGE won't help. Before he was arrested, he officially quit the group—and not on good terms. No one in the group is willing to risk everything to help him now."

"So there's no hope?" Fiola asked.

"Normally, I'd say no," Klar said, "but I think we're in luck. Hob is being held at the top of the guild's tower on the east side of Prima. Keen's wedding will be held on the twenty-ninth of Harkia in the west guildhall. It will be a big event, and most of the magicians and apprentices will attend. The east guildhall will be unusually empty. I'll be one of the few men there. I'm, uh, not exactly one of the grand magician's favorites. He didn't invite me to the wedding."

The wedding! Kaya jumped from her seat with excitement. She hadn't thought about it before, but now it seemed obvious. The wedding would provide a perfect diversion. "I can tell a story to make myself invisible. I did it before in Verdan to get into the guildhall there. Then I can sneak up to the top of the tower and free him."

She'd need the perfect story, one that would make Hob invisible too. Although, then she'd have a hard time finding him. She could come up with two stories, one for her and one for him.

"That won't work here," Klar said. "Prima has better security than Verdan. There's a spell protecting the perimeter of the east guildhall. Only a guild magician can pass without raising an alarm."

"Are you sure it's still active?" Fiola asked. "Hardly anyone in the guild can work spells anymore. Serves them right, too, after what they did to those poor creatures. Not you, of course."

Klar nodded. "I agree that the guild deserves its trouble. But there are enough guild members still favored by the listeners to work a few spells, and the perimeter is considered a priority. I wouldn't count on it being down."

Kaya sat back down, her excitement waning. "Can you undo the protective spell?"

"Not without raising more suspicion than I would like," Klar said.

In other words, he *could*, but he wouldn't. "Then what's the point of telling me where Hob is and when he'll be left unguarded?" Kaya demanded, her voice rising with each angry syllable. "What's the point of telling me any of this if I can't get to him?"

Miker started crying. Fiola picked him up. "Hush, hush," she said to the baby. "Everything's fine."

"No, it isn't!" Kaya yelled, causing Miker to wail louder in response.

"I have an idea for how you can get in," Klar said, and while Fiola worked to calm Miker, Klar proceeded to explain his plan.

Chapter Twenty-Seven

No one spoke for a while after Klar had finished.

Finally, Fiola broke the silence. "You can't expect Kaya to sneak into the guild like that. It's too dangerous. She's only a child. Why don't you just release Hob? You'll be there already."

"That's asking a lot of me, Fiola. I don't even know this boy. And from what I hear, his crimes aren't the kind to evoke leniency—" He hesitated, looking uneasily at Kaya. "If the guild finds out that I'm helping, I'll be executed too. While he's breaking out, I need to be with the other guild members, putting on a show of raising the alarms."

"Then *I'll* do it," Fiola said, crossing her arms.

"I don't think you'd fit through the passageway Kaya's going to use. Besides, what would happen if you got caught? Would you really leave Miker without a ma?" He gestured to the boy, who was still playing with his blocks, happily oblivious to the conversation.

"No," Fiola admitted. "You're right. It's too dangerous—for any of us."

"I can do it," Kaya said, finally finding her voice. "He's my brother. I'll do it. I have to."

Fiola took her niece's hand. "No, you don't. I understand that you love your brother. He loves you, too, which is why he wouldn't want you to risk your own life on some foolhardy attempt to rescue him." A tear rolled down her cheek as she squeezed Kaya's hand. "You can stay here, with me and Miker. I know you'll miss him, but it's for the best."

Kaya pulled her hand away. "He's always taken care of me. I owe him everything. You don't have to help me, but I won't stay here, knitting booties and enjoying myself, while he's executed."

She stood up. She looked around for her things, then realized she didn't have anything. There were some coins in her pocket from the scarves, booties, and rustberries she'd sold, but that was all. It would have to be enough. She walked to the door.

"Where are you going?" Fiola demanded. Miker stopped playing and started crying.

"I told you: I'm going to save Hob. I won't stay here, and you can't make me. You're not my ma. I barely even know you."

"Don't be silly." Fiola scooped up Miker again and rocked him back and forth to soothe him. "You can't save Hob tonight. The wedding isn't for four days. Spend that time here, working on the plan, building up your strength, and earning more coins."

That did sound better than spending the next few days on the streets. "You won't try to stop me?"

"I wish I could," Fiola said. "But I can see you got your ma's stubborn determination, so there would be no point." She used her sleeve to dry the tears from her cheeks. "I won't try to stop you. Just promise you'll stay for the next few days, please?"

"I promise," Kaya said.

When Kaya sat, Klar stood. "I should be going. MAGE is meeting at The Dirty Cup." Turning to Fiola, he asked, "Do you want to come?"

"I have my hands full." Fiola used her head to gesture toward Miker, now sleeping in her arms.

"You can bring him with you," Klar suggested. "You're always welcome."

Fiola smiled. "MAGE needs to keep a low profile, and Miker isn't always good at that. Thank you for your help tonight."

"Yes, thank you," Kaya said, but she eyed him with suspicion as he walked out the door.

—

After Klar left, Kaya held Miker while Fiola started dinner.

"Do you trust him?" Kaya asked.

"Who? Klar?"

"He's saying that Hob did something horrible, but I know Hob. He's a good person. He wants to help people. He wouldn't have done anything bad. What if Klar is lying? What if he's setting me up?"

"I trust him," Fiola said flatly. "He's not setting you up. Why don't you put Miker down and set the table? The stew will be ready soon."

Kaya put Miker down, but she didn't set the table. "I'm not hungry. I need to go on a walk, clear my head. I'll be back soon."

Fiola put down the spoon she was using to stir the stew. "Oh, I don't think that's a good idea. It will be getting dark soon. Maybe things were different in Verdan, but Prima can be quite dangerous, especially these days—"

"I survived on my own in the forest for days. I think I can handle an evening stroll."

"I'm just trying to look out for you."

"I don't need you to!" Kaya snapped, then regretted it. "Sorry. I just want some fresh air. I'll be back soon."

Fiola nodded. "I'll save some food for you."

Kaya hurried out. She felt guilty, but it wasn't because she'd snapped at her aunt. It was because she'd lied to her. She was not interested in an evening stroll. Klar had said MAGE was meeting at The Dirty Cup. Kaya had seen a sign for the restaurant near Amila's store. She headed in that direction.

The sun was almost finished setting. The streets were dark and menacing—they reminded her of the Shadows back in Verdan. There were guards, but not enough to stop every mugging or assault that happened, and their presence only served to remind Kaya of the dangerous elements that lurked around every corner.

She looked around for The Dirty Cup. It should have been right there—or was it down another block?

"Kaya!" someone exclaimed. "Kaya, is that you? Where's Fiola?"

Kaya turned to the voice. It was Amila. She was with a well-dressed, somewhat plump man.

"Good evening, Amila," Kaya said. "Fiola's at home with Miker."

"Are you heading there now?" Amila asked. "I'm afraid you're going in the wrong direction. Finding your way around Prima must be quite the challenge. Perhaps we can accompany you."

"We're expected," the man said, speaking to Amila and sounding impatient.

"They can wait," Amila said, with a smile that reminded Kaya of a dog baring its teeth.

"I'm actually going to The Dirty Cup," Kaya said. "Just point me in the right direction, and I'll find my way."

Amila looked uncertain about this, but at the urging of her companion, she pointed to a spot one block down.

"Thank you," Kaya said, hurrying toward the restaurant.

It was crowded and noisy. Kaya scanned the tables. She wouldn't be able to recognize the members of MAGE—it wasn't like they'd be flashing the bit of yarn around their wrists—so she looked for Klar. There he was, sitting at a table with several other people: two other men in guild uniforms, one boy in an apprentice's outfit, an elderly couple, three younger women, and two children.

She approached the table.

Klar noticed her. "What are you doing here? Is Fiola with you?"

One of the young women scooted to the side, but Kaya remained standing. "I came alone. I need to know more about Hob. He didn't do anything horrible." She met eyes with the other people at the table. "Why won't MAGE help him?"

Everyone at the table looked very uncomfortable. Klar stood and moved close to Kaya. In a low voice, he said, "No one here knows Hob, and you're announcing things that need to be kept quiet. We can talk more, but not here. Come with me."

Kaya followed him outside.

"Now, what do you need to know?" Klar asked.

"Why won't MAGE help Hob? The real reason. He didn't do anything horrible."

"You believe that, don't you?" He hesitated. "I told you everything I know, but I might have something that could help you."

He fished something out of his pocket and placed the small item in Kaya's hand. It was cold and hard, with one rounded end and one irregular end—a key.

"You'll need it to open Hob's cell," he said. "I thought about giving it to you before, but I feared what would happen if the guild learned I had lost mine. When you're done, hide it under the loose stone by the window."

Kaya put the key in her pocket. "If anyone catches me with it, I'll say I stole it."

"You should get home. Fiola must be worrying about you. She cares about you, you know."

Kaya nodded, although she couldn't help thinking it was rather silly. Walking around Prima might have been dangerous, but it was nothing compared to sneaking into the guildhall.

—

Over the next few days, Kaya spent most of her time knitting. She kept two blankets for herself, but she sold everything else at Amila's store. She and Hob would need all the coins they could get to start a new life.

The apartment was always filled with Miker's laugher, Fiola's stories, and the scent of fresh herbs. Even better, Fiola talked about her sister, Kaya's ma.

"She's the one who taught me story magic," Fiola said. "We used to sneak out of bed at night to tell stories. She was the best older sister a girl could have."

Under any other circumstances, the days would have been nice. But as it was, every second passed slowly, while each day passed too quickly. Soon, it was the twenty-ninth of Harkia, the day of the grand magician's wedding. The time had come for Kaya to rescue her brother—or else.

When the sun rose, Kaya rose with it. She was going over the stories she would need to tell, and she was only vaguely aware of Fiola getting up and busying herself in the kitchen, with Miker always at her feet.

"I've made baked crabapples for breakfast," Fiola said, "with some boiled eggs. I wanted to make bread, but the store I go to was out of grain."

The crabapples smelled delicious, but Kaya had no appetite. "Just leave it for me. I'll have it later, after you've left."

"Left? Where do you think I'm going?"

"Amila's shop," Kaya said. "You're going back, aren't you?"
Kaya would be there every day, if she were in Fiola's place.
There were too many coins to be made not to go.

"Not today. I'm going with you."

"You are? But you won't fit. And Miker—"

"I don't mean I'm going into the east guildhall, but I'll
accompany you as far as I can. Now please eat your breakfast.
You'll need your strength today."

Kaya ate quickly. The crabapple was sweet, and the eggs
were filling.

If the guild caught her, this could be the last decent meal
she ate. She wondered what Hob had been eating. Nothing
nearly so good, she imagined.

"It's not too late to change your mind," Fiola said.

"I can do this," Kaya said, trying to sound more confident
than she felt. She didn't want Fiola to worry.

Kaya would have felt at least a little better about her
chances if she'd had some conjuring incense, but Fiola never
used it, and Klar hadn't offered any. It was strange that the herb
attracted the invisible beings, she realized. She'd always taken
it for granted before, but now she wondered why it worked. It
smelled good, certainly, but did the listeners even have noses?

"What are they?" she asked.

"The listeners?" Fiola asked, and Kaya nodded. "No one
knows for sure. Some think they might be the spirits of a race
that lived on the planet before us. Others think they are us—
the ghosts of our dead. Most people think they're from another

world, guardians here to save us from ourselves. All we know for sure is that they're powerful and kind. They're our friends. Do we need to know more than that?"

"I suppose not." But it would have been nice. Kaya hesitated. "If Hob and I find a way, did you mean what you said? Can we really stay with you?"

"Yes." She put a plate of mushed crabapples in front of Miker and helped him grab his spoon. "We'll be one happy family," she added, smiling kindly.

"What about Klar?"

Fiola coughed. "Klar? What about him?"

"I saw the way you two looked at each other. Are you going to marry him?"

"We're that obvious, are we? His wife died around the same time my husband did. We've comforted each other, but I don't think either of us is ready to think about remarrying. Not right now."

"You should," Kaya said. "You make each other happy."

Kaya pictured everyone—herself, Hob, Miker, Fiola, and Klar—living as one big family. It would never happen, though. Klar and Fiola might marry, and they'd be happy with Miker and all their future children, but Hob and Kaya would never join them. Even if the day went as planned—a big if—there was no way they'd be able to stay in Prima.

And if things didn't go as planned . . .

Kaya didn't want to think about that. Instead, she focused on the stories she would tell. To have any chance of succeeding, she would need a great deal of magic on her side.

Chapter Twenty-Eight

As promised, Fiola accompanied Kaya to a small lake located near the east guildhall, right where Klar had told them to go. A gently flowing river, which served as Prima's main source of water, fed into the lake.

"Somebody might see you," Kaya warned.

"Let them see me," Fiola said. Miker tugged on her hair, eliciting a warm smile from her. "This area is open to anyone in Prima. I have every right to be here."

Perhaps. But Kaya would be continuing on to places strictly forbidden to non-guild members. "If I get caught and someone remembers seeing you with me shortly before, you could be questioned."

"If you get caught, you'll have bigger concerns than that. And I don't mind the guild questioning me. They've done it before. As long as you don't mention me, the guild will have no proof that I was involved, and Miker and I will be safe."

Kaya nodded. "I won't mention you."

"I'd prefer you didn't get caught." She looked over her shoulder. "No one is watching now, but that may change. You should hurry. There's a listener around. Two, if I'm not mistaken."

Kaya could feel the tingling. "What if there are no listeners to help me later?" she asked, still worried about the lack of incense—not that it would be much use after the swim she was about to take.

"They're here now. Simply ask them to stay close. Only magicians who try to bully the listeners need incense to lure them back."

Kaya wasn't sure she believed that. Hob used incense all the time. The listeners were fond of Fiola, so they took care of her, but that didn't mean they'd extend the same courtesies to anyone else.

Maybe they'd help today as a favor to Fiola. Kaya certainly hoped so.

"Listeners, I have a story that may interest you," she said, feeling awkward about using the formal, guild-based introduction in front of Fiola, but unsure of how else to start. "And I'll have more stories today, so please stick around. I'd really appreciate it. So, uh, the story.

"There once was a girl who lived on a small island. The island had plenty of food for her to eat and a cave for shelter, but there was one thing it lacked: companionship. She was alone on the island, and this made her sad."

"But even though she was alone on her island, she was not alone in the world. There were creatures in the water surrounding her island. They had fins instead of legs and gills on their necks. The girl gave them gifts of fruit that she harvested and pretty baubles that she made. The creatures sometimes crawled onto the beach to take these gifts, but they never stayed for long.

"If they would not stay with her, she wanted to stay with them. The girl tried to join them in the water, but even though she was a good swimmer, she quickly ran out of air and had to return to the surface.

"Meanwhile, her island was changing. Every day, the waves washed more and more of the land away. In a matter of weeks, there would be nothing left. If the girl could not find a way to survive underwater, she would die.

"One day, when very little of her island remained and all the fruit trees had been washed away, she had an idea. 'Help me survive underwater,' she begged the creatures. Together, they designed a device that allowed her to breathe underwater. With this device, she was able to stay in the water for as long as she wanted. She followed the creatures to their underwater home, a beautiful city with gleaming towers made of seashells and surrounded by forests made of kelp, and she lived there happily forever, never alone again."

Kaya hesitated. Fiola was giving her an odd look.

"Was the story good enough?" Kaya asked.

"It was fine," Fiola said. "But you don't have to worry about being alone. You'll always have family right here, with Miker and me."

Kaya knew Fiola meant what she said, but she also knew that she couldn't stay there. She wasn't alone. She had a brother—and he needed rescuing. She addressed the listener. "Help me survive underwater. Please."

"Good luck," Fiola said.

"Thank you," Kaya said. "For everything."

She was finally going to see her brother, but rescuing him meant leaving Fiola. It was a cruel trade-off, but there was nothing that could be done about it. She stepped into the water.

—

From above, the river appeared to end in a small lake. From the water, it was clear that the river continued beyond the lake, but it did so underground, through an opening in the otherwise solid rock that lined the lake.

Kaya swam into this opening.

It should have been cold, but Kaya did not shiver. She didn't struggle to breathe, either, as there was always a bubble filled with air at her lips. It should have been pitch black, but she could see. Beings of dazzling light swam beside her, imbuing the water with warmth.

Fiola had been right. Two listeners had been around to hear Kaya's story. Both of them accompanied her now.

The size of the underground tunnel varied. Sometimes Kaya barely managed to pass through the rocks, pulling herself forward more than swimming. At other times the passageway opened wide, leaving gaps between the surface of the water and the rocks above.

She scanned the ceiling of the underground river, in search of the well Klar had promised would be there. It led to the center of the guildhall and should be just large enough for a girl of Kaya's size to squeeze through.

And there it was—an unnaturally circular hole in the rock above her in one of the narrower parts of the underground river, where water filled every space available. She swam into the opening.

"Squeeze" had been the right word. She barely fit. If she got stuck, how long would the listeners supply her with air? Would they give her food too? How long could she survive?

She didn't want to find out. She pushed her way up. The sparkling listeners followed her.

Her head broke the water's surface, but she had not yet escaped the well.

It was good that the well was so narrow. Had it been wider, she couldn't have managed the climb up the smooth walls. As it was, she could keep her back against one side while her arms and legs thrust her upward.

When she reached the top, she wanted to wait before exiting—to listen for signs of guild members nearby—but her arms ached from swimming, and she could not hold her position for long. One more second, and she would slip back into the stream.

She climbed out of the well.

Chapter Twenty-Nine

Kaya found herself in a courtyard. Beyond the grass and trees, thick walls rose high into the air. There were several buildings too: solid stone structures decorated with carvings of the broad-leafed conjuring herb. It was not what she'd imagined—not at all like the single, massive structure back in Verdan—but there was no doubt that she'd reached the eastern guildhall.

So far so good . . . as long as she hadn't lost anything.

To check, she thrust her right hand into her skirt's pocket. Her fingers felt nothing other than wet cloth. The key must have fallen out during the swim. Which meant she'd already failed.

But no—the key was there, in the left pocket, next to her coin purse. She clutched the precious object but did not remove it.

The two blankets she'd knitted, currently wrapped around her shoulders like shawls, were drenched, and they did nothing to protect her from the chill. That was okay. She hadn't brought them for their warmth.

Thanks to the grand magician's wedding, the eastern guildhall should be nearly empty. Nearly. That was what Klar had promised. She didn't see anyone—and, hopefully, no one saw her—but that could change at any moment. She had to hurry.

Despite the existence of multiple buildings, her destination was obvious. Hob was being held in the tower, and that had to be the tall building that stood before her. She walked toward it.

Watery footprints marked each step she took. They were like an arrow, pointing to her, there for any guild member who happened to pass by.

That was a small problem compared to the next that arose.

The door to the tower wouldn't open. At first, Kaya thought it was merely heavy, but that wasn't the issue. It was locked. Klar had said it would be open.

She tried the key Klar had given her, even though it was supposed to be for Hob's cell, not the front door. Sure enough, the key didn't fit.

It was a snag in her plan, but she wasn't giving up so easily. There were other ways inside.

Did she have time for a story? Someone could appear any second.

Fiola had encouraged Kaya to ask the listeners for favors without telling a story. Kaya wasn't sure the listeners liked her enough to do this more than once or twice. What if she needed help later?

She decided to tell a story—a short one.

"Listeners," she whispered, "I have a story that may interest you. There once lived a girl made of wood. She was a doll, you see, but one made so well she came to life. The dollmaker had fashioned her a brain and placed it in a box in her head. He'd sealed the box too tight, though. As a result, the doll could not access the wisdom inside. She struggled, always making the wrong decisions, always needing others to guide her. One day, while trying to do something silly, she fell, and the fall caused the box to open just a crack. A single thought escaped, and it gave the doll an idea. 'Open,' she ordered the box in her head, and it did, and from then on she was very wise and always knew exactly what to do."

Kaya grimaced. Perhaps that had been *too* short. "Open," she said. "Please."

A strange breeze rose around her. It circled her before hitting the door—and the lock.

Kaya tried the knob. The door creaked open.

"Tharry?" a man's voice called. "Is that you?"

Kaya raced inside, closing the door behind her, and ducked beneath a large table covered with a tablecloth. From there, she took the opportunity to examine her surroundings. The staircase to her left must have led up to the tower. A door to her right led to another room, currently occupied by the man who thought he was talking to Tharry.

No one was passing. She stood—

And the door opened. She flung herself against the floor and scrambled back under the table.

Kaya couldn't see the man's face, just his guild-issued boots and clothes.

He paused in front of a wet footprint Kaya had left. Kaya wanted to tell another story, but she didn't dare speak, not even in a whisper. If the listeners could help her without requiring a story, this would be a wonderful time to do so.

The man stood there for a long time.

Kaya held her breath.

The man found her anyway. He lifted up the tablecloth and crouched down until his scarred face was almost level with Kaya's. His eyes stared right into hers.

It was Klar.

He winked. "Sorry I startled you. I was just coming to unlock the door, but I see you found your way in. You got here faster than I expected. Hob's up there." He nodded toward the stairs, where Kaya already knew she had to go, before returning the way he'd come.

Kaya scrambled up the stairs.

She'd gotten lucky, but the next time might be different. Klar had yelled to a man named Tharry, indicating the presence of another magician—one with no reason to help her. Kaya wanted to make it to the prison cells, but she'd rather not be thrown in one.

—

Kaya's legs ached in strange places. She was used to walking—more now than ever—but she had very little experience with stairs.

Verdan had a few steps scattered around the town. Belma's house in Silenton had a staircase too. This was different, though. These stairs went on and on, up and up.

Sometimes the steps stopped to make way for a door. Kaya paused at one, but she didn't try to open it. The prison cells were supposed to be at the top of the tower, and because more stairs remained, she knew she hadn't reached the top yet.

She was panting. Was she panting loudly enough to be heard on the other side of the heavy door? Sound wouldn't travel well through the thick stone, but the gaps between the door and the floor worried her.

While she stood there, attempting to determine whether anyone could hear her, the door opened.

Chapter Thirty

Kaya had nowhere to run. Up or down, it didn't matter. Either way, she'd be caught.

Her current position—standing behind the door as it creaked open, afraid the heavy stone would squish her—protected her only momentarily. The person who opened the door would enter the staircase, close the door, and see her.

"Listeners," she mouthed, not daring to make any sound. She had to do something, though. Perhaps the listeners could turn her invisible, as they had done once in Verdan. "I have a story—"

A loud thud interrupted her. About two floors below her, a small piece of wall had broken off and crashed into the stairs.

The magician—he had short black hair and a long beard—ran down to investigate. Kaya was in clear view now, but he wasn't looking at her.

Another chunk of stone wall plummeted to the floor, where it shattered against the steps just above the bearded guildsman. He ran out the door now nearest to him, a full two levels below Kaya's current position.

"Thank you," Kaya whispered, sure that the listeners had been behind this. She hurried up the rest of the steps.

The stairs ended. She'd reached the top of the tower.

—

She cracked the door open and peered into the room beyond. It looked empty. Completely empty. She didn't see any guild members on guard, nor did she see any prisoners. Most importantly, she saw no sign of Hob.

But this *was* the top of the tower. Hob had to be here—unless Klar had lied. No. At this point, even Kaya had to admit that seemed unlikely. He'd proven himself trustworthy several times over. But he could have been wrong about Hob's location. Or Hob could have been moved in preparation for the next day's execution. As Kaya thought about the possibilities, she realized just how many things could have gone wrong.

She stepped inside the empty room.

It was less empty than she'd realized.

The floor opened into a pit. It reminded her of the pit she'd seen near the guild's fields outside Verdan, the one used to trap hounds, only this was carved into the stone floor and topped with metal grates. It was also much larger, its diameter roughly equal to the height of three men. On one side, steep steps led to a hinged section of the grate, currently locked in place.

Hob sat inside, his arms tied behind his back. He was gagged, too, presumably so he couldn't tell a story.

She'd done it. She'd actually done it. She'd found her brother. Tears spilled down her cheeks, and her heart felt so full, so big, that she thought her chest would burst.

But it wasn't time to celebrate, not yet. Hob was still a prisoner.

Kaya didn't need a story, not this time. She had the key Klar had given her. It hadn't worked on the door to the tower, but it fit this lock perfectly.

Hob was staring wide-eyed at Kaya. He kept blinking, as if he wasn't sure of what he was seeing.

With the grate open, he began climbing out of the pit. Slowly. The steep steps were difficult to navigate with his hands tied behind his back, and his movements suggested weakness. The guild probably hadn't been feeding him well. Kaya felt guilty remembering her own delicious breakfast, and she wished she had brought something for him to eat.

She wanted to rush to him and hug him, but she worried she'd knock him back down into the pit. She waited for him to reach her. Then she removed the ropes binding his hands and the gag from his mouth. Finally, she hugged him.

"What are you doing here?" He looked at the key. "How did you get that?"

"Kl—" She stopped, worried that someone might hear. Besides, Hob probably didn't even know who Klar was. "All that matters is I'm here. I found you. But a guild member could come any second. We need to go."

She found the loose stone Klar had mentioned and tucked the key underneath it.

"How did you get in here?" Hob asked.

"Through the well, but I don't think you'll fit." The cramped space had barely allowed room for Kaya's passage, and she was much smaller than Hob, even though he had lost weight since last she'd seen him.

"I can tell a story to start a fire," Hob said flatly. "The guild can't stop us if they're burning."

Kaya gasped in horror. "But that would kill them! How can you want that? You're a member of the guild—or you were. You know they aren't all bad. Anyway, the listeners would never do it. They won't harm anyone. But it's okay. I have another plan. For once, *I'm* going to take care of *you*." She nodded toward the single window that lit the room. "You take one blanket, and I'll take another. I've thought up a story—"

"You want us to jump out the window on the strength of your magic? You've only told one story, and the bread burned, remember?"

"I've told many more since that," Kaya assured him. The window had no bars or glass, but it was too high to reach, and there was no furniture to climb. "I'll give you a boost, and then you can pull me up. I've prepared a story to help us fly."

"We're really going to jump?" Hob looked skeptical. "What if the listeners—"

"I trust them. Do you trust me?" She knelt down to give him a boost. His feet crushed her shoulders and smooshed her face, but he made it to the slight ledge. Then he yanked her up.

"Listeners," she said, speaking quickly, "I have a story that may interest you. There once was a girl who lived in the sky with her family and many friends. She had wings, as did the others of her kind, and she loved flying from cloud to cloud. Her days were filled with joy, and she had only a single worry.

"Evil wingless creatures lived beneath her. These creatures used to be able to fly, but their wings had been torn off, and this filled them with such pain and anger that they became wicked. They jumped up from the ground into the clouds and tried to grab the winged people. They would tear the wings off the people they caught, transforming them into evil creatures like themselves.

"The girl was careful to avoid the wingless creatures, but her little brother was not. One day, while he was napping on a particularly soft cloud, one of the creatures grabbed him.

"The girl saw this and flew down to rescue her brother. She was able to free him, but she was caught in the process. The evil creatures tore off her wings.

"The girl was hurt and angry, but she would not give up. She gathered feathers and twigs and fashioned them into a new pair of wings. 'Let these make flight possible,' she said, and when she flapped her new wings, she rose into the sky. She joined her friends and family, who praised her for her bravery and cleverness, and who said her wings were the most beautiful they had ever seen."

Kaya focused on her wet blankets. "Let these make flight possible. Please."

She gave one to Hob. Holding the other in her hands, she jumped.

The blanket spread out above her. She wasn't flying, not exactly, but she wasn't falling, either. She was gliding. A perfectly targeted wind kept her afloat. Above her, Hob hesitated at the window.

"It's fine!" she yelled. "Jump!"

Hob jumped. Then he plummeted.

Within a second, he was already far below Kaya and falling fast.

At this rate, the impact would kill him.

"Listeners!" Kaya screamed. "Let these make flight possible! Let these make flight possible! You have to help him! Please!"

His descent slowed. He was gliding, not as smoothly as Kaya, but well enough. When he reached the ground, he thudded against it painfully, but not lethally.

Kaya stepped gently onto the ground, like a bird alighting on a branch.

"I told you the listeners couldn't be counted on," Hob grumbled, rubbing his shoulder.

"They got us out, didn't they?" Kaya looked around to see exactly where they had landed. They were outside the gates, but only barely. In the distance, Klar could be heard yelling to the other guild members, raising the alarms—too late—just as he'd said he would. "We should hurry."

"I know just where we need to go," Hob said.

Kaya thought about objecting. She knew Prima better than he did, after all, since he'd spent all his time there trapped in a prison cell. But he seemed to know what he was doing, and he was her big brother. She followed him.

Chapter Thirty-One

Kaya wrapped her blankets around her head, partially concealing her face. It would have looked strange for Hob, a young man, to do the same, so he had to settle for keeping his head down.

With the help of the afternoon sun, Kaya's clothes went from wet to merely damp.

She wanted to tell Fiola she was okay, but they were headed in the wrong direction. It was probably for the best. She'd never promised to check in, and contacting Fiola now could prove dangerous. What if the guild was following Kaya? What if they suspected enough to keep an eye on Fiola?

Hob had a plan. Kaya just had to stick with him. From now on, whatever happened, she'd have him. Nothing else mattered.

—

They'd circled the same area—a block on the less-than-reputable edge of Prima—several times.

"What are we looking for?" Kaya asked.

Hob didn't respond for several minutes, long enough for Kaya to assume he never would. But then he finally answered. "This. This is what we're looking for."

It was a small inn, dark and dirty, the sort of establishment that made The Crusty Loaf back in Verdan look fancy. A woman stood behind the counter, and a few men sat at tables. Stairs led upstairs, to the guest rooms. "Why? What's here?"

"Not much, but they won't ask questions. Do you have any money?"

She handed over the coins she'd earned selling booties, scarves, and rustberries, along with a few more Fiola had given her. He took them and approached the woman behind the counter. She was middle aged, and her brightly colored clothes looked well made. Kaya suspected she owned the place.

After a short exchange, the woman gave Hob a key. He sat at a table and gestured for Kaya to join him. "We're going to get some food—I'm starving—and then we'll sleep here. I sent a message for Grey to meet us."

"Grey? He fled after the guild took you. I don't think he'll help." He hadn't helped Kaya, aside from warning her that the guild was after her.

"He will. We promised to meet up, in case something like this happened." Hob looked like he was about to say more, but right then, the woman appeared with big bowls of stew and an entire loaf of bread. Hob didn't bother with the spoon offered to him. He held the bowl like a cup and chugged the stew without chewing. Then he grabbed the loaf and, instead of tearing off a piece, proceeded to eat the entire thing.

Kaya didn't mind the lack of manners. The guild must not have been feeding him well. Of course he was eating like an animal. Besides, as worried as she was, she didn't think she could stomach much food. She nibbled at the vegetables in her bowl. Eventually, Hob took what was left, and that was fine with her.

They went up to their rented room. Hob slept while Kaya stared at the door and peered out the window, wondering how long it would take the guild to find them.

—

Hob slept for a long time, which surprised Kaya. He should have had plenty of sleep in the guild's prison, although maybe the quality hadn't been good enough to count. Regardless, she thought he'd be eager to move—to flee.

He rose long after the sun the next day.

"Fetch some breakfast for us," he said, stretching his obviously sore arms and legs.

"I gave all my coins to you," she said, so he fished a couple from his pants pocket and returned them to her.

Downstairs, the same woman, wearing a different but equally bright dress, was working behind the counter. She smiled kindly. Kaya almost asked for her name but caught herself just in time. If she asked the woman for her name, the woman would ask for Kaya's name in response, and the last thing she wanted to do was identify herself.

Indulging in as little conversation as possible, Kaya exchanged some of the money for bread, cheese, and water. She did not say anything about the price, even though it seemed high. Everyone was charging more these days, she supposed, assuming they could even find grain to make bread. Regardless, complaining wouldn't do any good. Grateful for the coins in her purse and the food in her hands, Kaya hurried back to the room.

"What do we do now?" she asked Hob. "We need to come up with a plan. I was thinking—"

"I already told you." His words were muffled by a mouthful of bread. "We wait for Grey."

"But why?" she insisted. "Shouldn't we be getting as far away from the guild as possible? We can't go back to Verdan—they'd look for us there—but we could try a town to the east."

Hob shook his head. "We're not running. The guild thinks they have all the power, but they're wrong. The listeners have the power, and we have the listeners."

Kaya didn't feel their presence. She'd barely felt it at all since their jump from the tower, except for a few tingles while she was fetching breakfast. "We can't fight the guild."

"The guild won't be around much longer," Hob said. "We have a plan."

"Who has a plan?" Kaya asked. "You and Grey? Is MAGE involved?"

"No. MAGE is too afraid to help. It's just Grey and me."

"Klar—that's Aunt Fiola's friend . . . well, maybe more than her friend . . . Anyway, they helped me plan your rescue, but Klar said MAGE wouldn't help because you'd done something horrible. I told him he had to be wrong, because you would never do anything bad. If we tell him and Fiola your plan, they can talk to the others at MAGE, and—"

"No," Hob interrupted. "MAGE doesn't understand."

"So tell *me*. I'll understand."

He shook his head. "I won't *tell* you. I'll *show* you. Just as soon as we hear from Grey."

Chapter Thirty-Two

Hob spent the next two days eating and sleeping. Kaya forced herself to eat and tried to make herself sleep, but worrying occupied most of her time.

When she went downstairs to fetch food, she always dealt with the same woman. Renting rooms and taking food orders didn't seem to require much of her time. She looked bored, and sometimes she chatted to Kaya about the weather or something else trivial.

"It's gotten really cold, hasn't it?" she'd say. "We might even see snow soon."

Or she'd comment on a bird she'd seen recently. "They've normally all migrated by this time of year."

Kaya muttered responses before running away. It was better not to talk to anyone, just in case she let something slip.

Unless her reticence made her more suspicious.

She missed talking to Anny. She missed Fiola and Miker, too, even though she hadn't known them long. Their home had been full of warmth and laughter, and the same could not be said for the rented space she was staying in now. If only she'd been able to accept Fiola's offer to stay with them.

But it was too late for that. Hob had needed her, and now they both needed to stay hidden.

She thought she'd be happy, once she had her brother to take care of her again, but she wasn't. He seemed even less kind than she'd remembered. Had his time as a prisoner changed him?

Maybe if they talked, things could go back to normal. Hob was sitting at the small table in their room, on a wobbly chair that threatened to collapse under his weight, and he appeared lost in thought.

"How are you doing?" Kaya asked.

He didn't respond right away, as if it took him a moment to register that someone was talking to him. An expression of confusion flashed on his face before settling into anger. "How do you think? You saw the guild's prison. It was awful. They barely fed me, you know."

"I know," Kaya said. "I'm sorry it took me so long. I had to walk all the way from Verdan, and then I had to—"

"Don't worry about it," Hob interrupted. "I'm not mad."

Kaya's mouth fell open.

He wasn't *mad*? About taking too long to rescue him? Kaya had meant what she said—she was sorry the journey had taken so long, that Hob had to suffer in the guild's prison for all that time—but this had more to do with pity than apology. She had suffered too.

She'd expected gratitude, not forgiveness.

Unless he wasn't talking about how much time she'd taken to rescue him, but about needing rescuing in the first place. "Do you mean you're not mad that the guild found out I could do story magic? I know I shouldn't have done it in public, but those boys were mugging me, and I was scared and angry. I'm so sorry. It was all my fault. I won't do magic anymore. I won't have to, now that you're—"

"What? No. Don't be silly. What happened to me had nothing to do with you. It was something else. Something important."

"But Grey said—"

Someone knocked on their door. How loudly had she been talking just then, when she'd confessed to practicing story magic and mentioned her brother's arrest by the guild?

Too loudly.

The knocking repeated. It wasn't regular knocking. It had a rhythm to it.

"It's Grey," Hob said. "Let him in."

—

They didn't kick Kaya out of the room, but only because they were too busy ignoring her. She tried to follow their conversation, carried out in grave, hushed tones. Little of it made sense to her.

"Did the guild find them?" Hob asked.

Find what?

"No," Grey said. "I hid them in a spot outside the city."

Hid what?

"Do you have any with you now?" Hob asked.

Grey shook his head. "I wasn't sure what to expect here. I thought it might be a trap. How did you get out? I wanted to help, but I needed to keep a low profile, in case anyone was still looking for me. I thought about trying to sneak into the eastern guildhall anyway, but there was no way to do it without getting caught."

Hob gestured to Kaya—the first time he had acknowledged her since Grey arrived. "She did it."

"Your little sister? Wow. That's pretty lucky."

Kaya drew a sharp breath. "I walked all the way from Verdan. Then I swam into the eastern guildhall through their well. It took a lot of planning, and it was very dangerous. 'Luck' may have played a role, but there was a great deal more to it than that."

Grey laughed. "Whoa, calm down. I just meant it was lucky for Hob."

That hardly mollified Kaya. "What were the two of you talking about? You said you hid something outside Prima?"

Hob and Grey exchanged glances and nodded.

"Does it have anything to do with why the guild is after you?"

More glances and nodding, but no answers.

Kaya was growing tired of this. She eyed Grey. "You said the guild was looking for me—that it was my fault Hob had been taken. Why were you lying to me?"

Grey shrugged. "I wasn't sure I could trust you. I thought if you knew the truth, you might tell the guild where I was, try to use it as leverage to get Hob out. Not that it would have worked. The guild would have just arrested both of us."

"So what really happened?" Kaya demanded.

Hob eyed the door as if he suspected someone of listening on the other side. "We can't talk here."

—

"This is it," Grey said, before adding a less confident, "I think."

Kaya was thinking plenty of her own thoughts, namely that he was lost. She wished she could feel the reassuring tingling of listeners, but she'd barely sensed them in days, and she didn't have any incense to summon them.

"Where?" Hob asked, looking up at the trees.

Grey pointed to the ground. "We have to dig." He approached a bush, reached his hand inside, frowned, then smiled as he pulled out a shovel. "I knew this was the right spot."

There was only the one shovel, so he dug a hole while Kaya and Hob watched. And watched. And waited. Whatever Grey had hidden, he'd buried it deep.

Something pricked Kaya's neck. She swatted at her hairline, expecting to find a swarm of insects, but there was nothing there.

It wasn't just her neck. Her arms, her back, her legs—her entire body stung.

The pain was strange but familiar.

"The hounds!" she screamed. "The guild's hounds are here."

"How do you know about the hounds?" Hob asked.

"I—" She stopped. Explaining would take too long. "It doesn't matter right now. They're close. Can't you feel them?"

"It's not the hounds. It's this." Grey held up a small metal container.

Chapter Thirty-Three

"**W**hat is it?" Kaya asked. The container was about the size of her first. It wasn't metal, as she'd first thought, but pottery painted with a metallic sheen. When she shook it, she heard the whooshing sound of water inside.

Grey removed several more from the hole. "They're listeners."

Kaya dropped the container. It landed on a small pile of fallen leaves, which kept it from shattering. She picked it up again and examined it. "How is that possible?"

"It's complicated," Hob said, taking one of the containers from Grey. "You don't know enough about listeners to understand—"

"You tricked them into becoming water-bound and trapped them inside these containers," Kaya interrupted, figuring it out. "The paint contains barrier metal to trap them inside, or else the metal is in the pottery itself."

Hob nearly dropped his container. "How do you know that?"

"I know a lot. I've learned a lot. Rescuing you wasn't easy." She picked up the container. Her fingers stung at its touch. "You're torturing them."

"Don't be silly," Hob said. "They're listeners, not people. They're here to serve us, and we shouldn't have to tell stories to make them do it."

"We don't *have* to tell stories. We tell them stories because they like them, and they're our friends, but they'll do magic for us without stories, when we really need it, if we're nice to them."

"No, they won't, not when they're free, not unless they're forced. And even when we tell stories, they won't always do what we need. That's why we need a new way to control them. Don't look so angry." Hob laughed. "This is why I didn't tell you about the containers earlier. I knew you wouldn't understand. It's not your fault. You don't know enough about magic."

Kaya thought she knew plenty. More than she used to. Maybe even more than her brother, she was beginning to realize. Because listeners *did* perform magic without stories. She'd seen it before, when the stone fell in the stairwell and when the rustberries grew out of season. And so what if they did demand stories as payment most of the time? Most people demanded more than a bit of entertainment for their labor. It was no reason to torture the listeners.

This was torture, no matter what Hob said.

Listeners didn't like being trapped. That was why their normally pleasant tingles had turned painful. The listeners were scared. They were begging for help. They were lashing out.

Kaya felt sick at the thought of what she was holding. "These containers are no better than the hounds."

"Of course they are," Grey said. "The guild made a mistake using living animals. They thought they could train the dogs, but it just added a layer of unpredictability. These containers are simple. They're easy to control."

"Think about all the good we can do," Hob said. "The grand magician heard we had a new way of controlling the listeners. He was desperate to find out what it was, but I wouldn't tell him. Once Grey and I make enough of these, we can overthrow the guild. Then we can do everything the guild refused to do— grow more food, heal the sick, whatever we want. The guild let our parents die because they didn't think healing them was worth their time. We could be kinder. We could be better."

He had a point. When Kaya had helped that boy with the infected leg, she'd seen firsthand that story magic could heal, even if it couldn't heal everyone. And if the guild stopped growing conjuring herb, all that land could be used to grow food. More people could eat. Fewer people would suffer.

But this wasn't the way. It wasn't better—it was torture. She could feel the listeners' pain, the way it radiated from them and stabbed at her skin. The barrier metal hurt them. If the listeners remained trapped for too long, they'd become as twisted as the hounds.

All the good Hob wanted to accomplish could be done without the cruelty of these containers.

"You told MAGE, didn't you?" Kaya said, remembering what Klar had told her. Hob had done something so horrible that MAGE had turned against him. She hadn't believed it at the time. "You told them about the jars, and they were horrified. They wanted nothing to do with you. One of them probably said something to the guild. That's how the grand magician found out."

Hob's face burned with anger. "They're childish. They want the world to match some ideal they've dreamed up, and when it doesn't, they give up."

"They'll learn," Grey added. "When they see us take over, they'll be sorry."

When that happened, Kaya thought, a lot of people would be sorry.

But why hadn't it happened yet?

"If these containers make you so powerful, why haven't you overthrown the guild yet?" Kaya asked. "How did they capture you?"

"Well," Hob began, his tone turning defensive, "we haven't gotten the listeners to do what we say yet. They're still resisting. It's only a matter of time, though. We just have to break them."

Yes!

That was it, Kaya realized. She had to break them.

Just not in the way Hob meant.

She threw the container she was holding on the ground and stomped on it. The container broke into several large shards. Hob yelled at her, and Grey let out a stream of curses and insults, but she ignored both of them. The listener that had been trapped inside gained instant freedom. It was no longer bound to the water, which now formed a muddy puddle at Kaya's feet, so she couldn't see it, but she felt a burst of relieved tingles when it escaped.

The other listeners remained trapped, though, and Kaya could feel them too. She had to free them all. If this required going against Hob and Grey, so be it. She'd faced worse challenges on her journey to Prima. She wasn't as weak as she'd once been.

Ready to fight if it came to that, she stepped toward Hob and the containers behind him. He spread out his arms, making himself as big as possible to block her. He looked ready to fight too.

A shrill note stopped her in her tracks. She spun around and saw exactly what she had feared.

A member of the guild was staring at them, a whistle in his mouth.

Chapter Thirty-Four

The man's gray hair and lined face marked him as an older member of the guild, though his plain uniform made his low rank clear. It didn't matter. He belonged to the guild. With wrists free of yarn, he did not belong to MAGE.

He didn't move forward, but he didn't back away, either. "Several other guild magicians are on their way. You can try to run, but you won't get far."

"Listeners," Grey said, "I order you to stop this man."

The listeners did nothing.

"Kill him!" Grey yelled. "I order you!"

The listeners did not respond.

"They won't kill," Kaya said. "Not ever."

Except that wasn't true. The hounds killed. If these listeners suffered much more, they might become violent too—but then they would never take commands.

"Then stop him some other way," Hob said. "Listeners, tie him up with vines. Trap him in a pit the way they imprisoned me."

The listeners didn't.

The man blew his whistle again, but he refused to budge, despite the threats.

The freed listener had stuck around. It was hard to feel, its presence nearly drowned out by the pain of the trapped listeners, but Kaya could sense it if she focused. It was there, she guessed, because it wouldn't abandon the others of its kind. Against the barrier metal in their containers, it was helpless, so it simply stayed there, watching, waiting.

"Listener," Kaya whispered so the guild magician couldn't hear her words. Not that it mattered at this point. Getting caught for story magic was the least of her concerns. "Listener, I know you're angry. You want to free your friends, and I do too. I will, I promise, but first I need your help."

"What are you doing?" Hob demanded.

"What you taught me," she said, although she'd been hoping story magic would prove unnecessary, that the listener would choose to help because Kaya had freed it. Upset as she was, she didn't think she could tell a proper story.

She'd have to try.

"Listeners, I have a story that may interest you. There once lived a girl—"

Grey rushed the magician. They both landed a few punches before tumbling to the ground. They wrestled for a few minutes, fingers poking eyes, nails tearing skin, hands strangling necks. Grey fought like the street boys back in Verdan.

Then Grey rose. The guildsman did not.

"Is he okay?" Kaya asked, sure that he wasn't. The man didn't move.

"He's alive," Grey said, kicking the man in the stomach.

"You'd better leave him that way," Hob said. "He might have been telling the truth about other magicians being close behind. We don't need to give them another reason to hunt us down."

Kaya couldn't believe her ears.

Hob didn't want to kill the guildsman—because it wasn't convenient. Not because it was wrong. Not because he cared.

Grey returned to the hole he'd dug. He threw Hob four containers and kept four for himself. "I think this is about all we can carry, unless you think your sister can be trusted with them."

Hob glared at her. "No. We'd better leave the rest."

In the distance—but not that distant—voices echoed through the trees. More men were coming.

"Listeners, stop those magicians," Grey commanded.

The listeners ignored him.

"You started telling a story to the freed listener," Hob said. "Is it still around?"

Kaya hesitated, not sure she wanted to help her brother. "Yes."

"Listeners," he said, "I have a story that may interest you. There once—" His story dissolved into screams. "It's attacking me! Help! It stings! It burns!"

Why shouldn't the listener attack? Hob had tortured the poor creature, and now he requested favors. Stories weren't enough anymore, not after what he'd done.

Grey grabbed Kaya's arm. "You can do it. When you started your story, they didn't attack. You have to help us."

The already-not-that-distant voices were drawing nearer.

"Please," Hob begged.

Kaya couldn't bear to look at him. Facing the ground, she said, "Listeners, I have a story that may interest you. When it's done, I'll free the others. I promise. One day, long ago, a bear found a baby girl in the forest. The bear was hungry, and it wanted to eat the baby. But before it could sink its teeth into her flesh, the baby laughed, and the bear's heart melted. It decided to raise the baby.

"The bear kept the baby in its cave, where she was warm and safe. But the baby grew up, and although she loved the bear dearly, she did not want to stay in the dark cave forever. Although the bear had warned her about the dangers of the forest, she decided to risk venturing outside. She waited until the bear was out, because she did not want it to worry, and then left.

"The forest was not at all what she'd imagined. She loved the bright sunlight and the beautiful flowers. Most of all, she loved the animals. The bear had taught her that all animals were frightening, but she quickly made friends with a gentle deer.

"She had such fun that she didn't realize how late it had gotten. The bear returned. It attacked the deer and killed it.

"The bear tried to get the girl to return to the cave, but she refused. The bear realized that the deer had been her friend. The bear begged for forgiveness, but the girl was too angry to forgive the bear, and she never wanted to return to the cave. When the bear promised to do anything to make her happy again, there was only one thing she wanted. 'Go away,' she said, and the bear left, heartbroken, never to be seen again."

"I think I see the guildsmen coming," Hob said. "Wait until all of them are in sight before making them go away. We don't want to get rid of some and have to deal with rest ourselves."

Kaya saw them too. She had to hurry. "Do you promise never to make these containers again?"

"But we need—"

"I won't do it unless you promise. The containers don't work. The listeners will never obey you, not like this. And it's cruel. It's torture. Promise you won't make the containers again."

"Fine," Hob said. "I promise. I'll figure out a better way. You'll see."

Kaya shook her head. "I'm not going with you." Eyeing both Hob and Grey, she said, "Go away."

Chapter Thirty-Five

Hob and Grey vanished. Kaya didn't know where they went. All she knew was that she could no longer see or hear them.

One by one, she stomped on the containers, including the ones Hob and Grey had dropped when they disappeared. The jars broke into shards underneath her boots. Her skin tingled with the ecstatic relief of the listeners as they were freed. The guildsmen arrived just as she was stepping on the last one.

—

Of the six guildsmen, two tended to the man Grey had attacked, two searched the area for Grey and Hob, and two escorted Kaya back to the city.

One of the men was short and stout with a beard that reached his belly. The other had strange markings on his face, something Kaya had heard of before but had never seen. Tattoos, she thought they were called. He must have come from faraway lands.

Neither of them spoke as they led Kaya to the eastern guildhall. They went through the massive gates, of course, and not the well or the window.

Kaya did her best to look at the impressive buildings and the beautiful courtyard with awe in her eyes, as if she were seeing everything for the first time. No one had to know she'd sneaked inside only days before.

The courtyard was much busier than the last time she'd been there, when the grand magician's wedding had almost emptied the premises. Several magicians watched Kaya as she was led past the well. None of them were Klar.

She considered jumping down the well to try to escape that way, but the tattooed man gripped her wrist too tightly. She'd need to find another way out of this.

The two men did not take Kaya to the top of the tower as she had feared. Instead, they brought her to one of the smaller buildings, to a dimly lit room, and put her in a chair. They sat in front of her.

"Tell us what happened," the bearded man said. "Do not lie to us."

"We have ways of making people talk," the tattooed man added.

She was sure they did. "I heard Hob was being held here in Prima. I didn't know why. I came here to see if I could help. I didn't learn about the containers until he brought me into the forest today."

"And then you broke them," the bearded man said.

"They were horrible." In case the guildsmen got any ideas, Kaya quickly added, "And they didn't work."

"Where did Hob and Grey go?" the tattooed man asked. "Where are they now?"

"I don't know. They disappeared."

"You expect us to believe that?" The bearded man turned to his partner. "She could be the one who helped Hob escape."

The tattooed man laughed. "Come on, you can't actually think a little girl could have done that? Look at her!"

Kaya did her best to look meek and innocent.

"I agree," the bearded man said. "But she might have helped. Besides, she knows too much. We should execute her."

The tattooed man stood.

Kaya scrambled out of her seat and hurried to the door, but the man's legs were longer than hers, and he covered the distance in less time. He grabbed Kaya.

Then he screamed.

"What is it?" the bearded man asked. His confusion turned to anguish. He swatted at his arms, desperate to rid himself of an invisible attacker. "Something's stinging me!"

"It's the listeners," Kaya said. "They're protecting me. You can stop now, listeners, but stay close."

The two men relaxed. The listeners' assault on them had stopped.

"How did you get them to do that?" the bearded man asked. "The listeners don't hurt people."

"They don't like to cause harm, but they will protect the people they like," Kaya said. "And they like me. If you try to hurt me again, they'll get angry. I might not be able to stop them."

Kaya wasn't sure whether that was true, but she suspected that it was. These were the listeners she had freed. They were not as far gone as the hounds, but nor were they as gentle as most listeners. They might be dangerous when pushed.

Kaya opened the door. Neither man attempted to stop her. She was free to go—and Kaya knew exactly where she wanted to be.

Chapter Thirty-Six

Fiola welcomed Kaya with open arms, just as she'd said she would. She must have been expecting Kaya, too, or at least hoping, because she had already purchased the loom she'd offered.

A month later, Kaya had yet to master the loom, but she was making progress. She was working on material for a dress that, if it turned out half as well as she hoped, would make a nice outfit for herself. Then she'd start on something to sell in Amila's store.

Every time Kaya went there—or anywhere—guild members followed her. Klar said to ignore them. The guild was more afraid of her than she was of them. Kaya suspected he underestimated just how afraid she was.

At least the listeners were staying close by.

Miker let out a gleeful squeal as the tower of blocks he'd been playing with tumbled.

Kaya feigned shock. "What did you do, Miker?"

He burst into a fit of laughter.

The blocks reassembled themselves into a tower. That was how it appeared, anyway. Of course, a listener was responsible for the movement. Kaya watched for a moment, then returned her focus to the loom. Fiola had spent good money on it, and Kaya didn't want to let her down.

Someone knocked on the door.

"That will be Klar," Fiola said. She was by the stove, preparing dinner. Apparently, Klar had been invited to eat with them. Again. Kaya was always happy for his company, but she did worry that they wouldn't provide a large enough meal to satisfy a man of his size. Food was increasingly hard to find, even for people with money.

How would such a large city survive the winter with so little food? People were already starting to get hungry, desperate, violent—and winter had barely even begun.

But at least Kaya wouldn't have to face the lean winter alone. She smiled as she got up to open the door.

She gasped when she saw him.

Klar's left eye was bruised, and his lip was swollen. He entered, shutting the door behind him, though not before the wind blew a fine dusting of snow inside.

"What happened?" Kaya asked.

"What? Oh." Klar touched his lip gingerly. "This. It's nothing."

"Was it another uprising?" Fiola asked. Everyone knew how bad the streets had gotten. Kaya could walk safely, but that was only because the listeners she'd freed stayed by her side, protecting her. Others were not so lucky, and that included the guild members. It was becoming obvious that the guild could no longer control the listeners.

"Yes, but like I said, it's nothing. I need to tell you something—"

Someone knocked. A moment later, before anyone had a chance to respond, the door opened.

Fiola drew a sharp breath. "Keen Im'Trif!"

The grand magician. He was here, in the apartment—with a face more bruised than Klar's. Two guild members walked in behind him. Kaya recognized them as the bearded man and tattooed man, though she'd never learned their names.

"Are you Kaya?" he asked.

Kaya wanted to say no, but the guild had been following her for weeks. They knew who she was, and there was no point in lying. "Yes."

Fiola moved close to her, half-shielding her from the grand magician.

"Don't worry," Keen said. "I won't try to hurt you. I can feel the presence of the listeners, and I know they protect you. That's why I'm here. I want to know what you're doing to control them."

"I'm not controlling them," Kaya said. "I'm their friend."

Fiola smiled proudly.

"Is it the jars?" Keen continued, as if he hadn't heard her. "We made some, but the listeners still wouldn't obey us. It only seemed to make them angry—even angrier than they already were. What's your trick? Tell us now, or even the listeners won't be able to protect you."

Keen, the bearded man, and the tattooed man immediately looked uncomfortable. They swatted at their skin, as if something was stinging them.

"You're upsetting the listeners," Kaya said. "They don't like it when people threaten me."

"That wasn't a threat," Keen said, smiling and taking a step back. "Like I said, I'm not here to hurt you. But you must tell us your trick. For the good of Prima and the kingdom."

"The listeners won't help you, because you keep hurting them," Kaya said. "They help me because I'm their friend."

"Will you show us how you do it?" Keen asked. "You've seen the way Prima is suffering. Verdan is even worse. We can't grow enough food without the listeners."

"She's just a child—" Fiola started.

"I'll help you," Kaya interrupted.

The grand magician sighed with relief.

"On three conditions. First, you have to promise not to hurt the listeners again. No more barrier metal. No more trapping them. Second, you have to stop growing so much conjuring herb. You shouldn't need it, not if you know how to treat the listeners, and you can use the land to grow more food."

Keen nodded. "What is the third condition?"

"You can't tell any more lies about story magic, trying to make people think it's difficult or dangerous when you know it isn't. You have to teach story magic to anyone who wants to learn. Including girls."

Keen's eyes widened. "Girls can't do story magic!"

"I'm a girl," Kaya said. "And I'm not the one asking for help with listeners."

His face reddened. "But you're just *one* girl. Most can't do it. They simply don't have the capacity—"

"I manage fine," Fiola said. "And so did Kaya's ma. You'll find that there are many people, women and men, who have learned story magic. If you don't welcome us, you may find us fighting against you. Especially if things get as bad as you seem to think they will."

Keen was silent for a long time. When he spoke, all of the pomp and bluster had left his voice. "Your conditions are acceptable. How shall we start?"

"We'll figure that out tomorrow," Fiola said. "Right now, you're interrupting our dinner."

Klar showed the other guildsmen outside while Kaya dished out food for him, Fiola, Miker, and herself. It wasn't much, but it was the best meal she'd ever had.

Chapter Thirty-Seven

*T*he listeners weren't eager to help very many of the guild magicians, especially after their more recent experiments trying to copy Hob's jars, but they did as Kaya asked. Food grew, even though the ground was cold and the sky was gray. The sick healed, at least when their injuries and illnesses weren't beyond the listeners' powers. More and more people learned to tell stories. Slowly, the kingdom prospered.

Keen Im'Trif was still the grand magician, but in name only. He would never do story magic again. The listeners wouldn't let him. Kaya was in charge, and everyone knew it— Keen Im'Trif, most of all.

But Kaya was still only twelve, soon to be thirteen, and she knew little about politics and resource management. For that, and for so much more, she had Fiola.

It was exhausting work. By the time they walked home one evening, it was already dark. At least the streets were quiet. The crime and violence had died down as the food stores had replenished.

As they entered Fiola's apartment—their apartment—Miker let out an irritated cry.

"What's wrong?" Kaya asked. "Are you hungry?"

"He's cranky because he missed his nap," Fiola said. "Can you get dinner ready while I put him in his crib?" Singing a lullaby, Fiola carried him into the other room.

They had some flour, but it was far too late to start the bread—unless Kaya used magic. She began mixing the dough. As she did so, her thoughts turned to the first story she'd told, the one to make the bread rise.

She never would have done that if not for Hob. Despite everything that had happened, he was still her brother. She missed him terribly—when her anger didn't push out her more generous thoughts.

He was okay, wherever he was. Kaya wasn't sure what the listeners had done to him. They couldn't make things, or so Hob believed, but they could clearly make things disappear. Did they turn him invisible and whisk him away? Or instantly transport him to some faraway land? Regardless, Kaya trusted they hadn't hurt them. Not too badly anyway. They weren't like the hounds, and they wouldn't do anything to upset Kaya. Hob was safe.

But *where* was he safe?

"Listeners, I have a story that may interest you," she began out of habit. She knew the formality wasn't necessary. "Once, there was a nest, and in that nest, there were five eggs. One of the eggs cracked, and a chick emerged. She had hatched early, and her brothers and sisters would stay in their eggs for several more weeks. In that time, the mama bird fed the chick, and she grew big and strong.

"Then one day, the mama bird did not return. The chick was young, and she had never flown before, but as she grew hungry and scared, she decided she would have to try. She spread her wings, jumped out of the nest—and fell. But she didn't give up. She flapped her wings as hard as she could, and before she hit the ground, she felt herself rising into the air. She was flying.

"She found the mama bird, whose wings were broken and whose feathers were bloodied. The mama bird begged the chick to return to the nest to protect her brothers and sisters as they hatched.

"Heartbroken, the chick did as she was told. When she reached the nest, she saw a snake slithering away. It had eaten three of the eggs, leaving only one.

"The nest was not safe. The chick carried the remaining egg to the ground, a difficult task for the small bird, and buried the egg in a hole, where it would be warm and hidden and safe. Then the chick went out to find food.

"But when the chick returned, she could not find the spot where she had buried the egg. She had promised to protect her siblings, and she had failed. She cried.

"A worm emerged from the dirt. Normally, the chick would have eaten it, but she was too upset, so she let it be. The worm thought the chick must be kind to spare it, and when it saw that the chick was crying, it asked if it could help. 'Show me where my sibling is,' the chick said, and the worm found the egg, and the chick was able to fulfill her promise to the mama bird."

Kaya's own heart pounded. She might not like the answer she received. But she had to know. "Show me where my sibling is," she asked. "Please, show me my brother, where he is."

She didn't know how the listeners would do her bidding, if they even could. They were powerful beings, but invisible and silent. Perhaps this was beyond their ability.

The lump of dough flattened itself into a rectangle Kaya drew a sharp breath. The listeners had found a way to answer her question.

Lines emerged in the doughy rectangle. A map! A large X appeared last, marking a spot far to the south, past Verdan, past the lands controlled by the king and the guild, and into lands Kaya did not know the names of.

Maybe someday Kaya could forgive her brother, and then she would make another long journey, even longer than the last, to see him. It would be difficult, but she had the strength and the intelligence to succeed.

For now, though, her home was in Prima, with Fiola and Miker. And there was work to do. The guild needed Kaya. The entire kingdom did.

When she had finished kneading the dough, she told a story to make the bread rise. It worked—and even better than it needed to. The dough didn't merely double in size. It floated above the table.

This time, she didn't burn it.

Acknowledgments

In *Story Magic*, storytelling is the source of all magic. In the real world, we might say the same thing. Stories give us the chance to explore new worlds and new lives. How is that not magical?

Seeing *Story Magic* go from idea to manuscript to book has also been magical. I couldn't have done it on my own. I am forever grateful to Mari Kesselring and everyone at Jolly Fish Press and North Star Editions. Mari always seemed to know what I was trying to do with this story, even when I didn't quite know it myself yet. Now that's magic.

I also need to thank everyone who supported me along the way. I won't try to list names—there are too many, and I'm sure I'd leave someone out. Whether you gave me feedback on early drafts, helped me talk out my plot problems, listened to my rantings and ravings, or simply offered encouragement—thank you.

Finally, I must thank you, the reader. I hope you find something magical in this story.

About the Author

Laurel Gale is the author of *Dead Boy* and *Monster, Human, Other*. She lives with her husband and their ferrets in Washington. You can visit Laurel online at laurelgale.com or on Twitter at @laurel_gale.